"You're living in a fantasy world."

Rob spoke harshly. "You've always wanted to marry Clay because he shared your happy childhood. But your dream of future happiness included the farm. And now that the farm is mine—"

"I'm marrying Clay," Cathie broke in quickly, "because I love him."

"As a brother or a lover?" he asked.

Her reply was lost as Rob's mouth closed over hers, expertly arousing forbidden desires. It was torturous bliss—wanting him and despising herself for that wanting. When she thought she could no longer resist giving herself up totally to his embrace, he suddenly released her.

"Your dream belongs in the past, Cathie," he said huskily, his eyes darkening. "Don't fight me anymore. Not now—or ever."

JANET DAILEY AMERICANA

ALABAMA—Dangerous Masquerade
ALASKA—Northern Magic
ARIZONA—Sonora Sundown
ARKANSAS—Valley of the Vapours
CALIFORNIA—Fire and Ice
COLORADO—After the Storm
CONNECTICUT—Difficult Decision
DELAWARE—The Matchmakers
FLORIDA—Southern Nights
GEORGIA—Night of the Cotillion
HAWAII—Kona Winds
IDAHO—The Travelling Kind
ILLINOIS—A Lyon's Share
INDIANA—The Indy Man
IOWA—The Homeplace
KANSAS—The Mating Season
KENTUCKY—Bluegrass King
LOUISIANA—The Bride of the Delta Queen
MAINE—Summer Mahogany
MARYLAND—Bed of Grass
MASSACHUSETTS—That Boston Man
MICHIGAN—Enemy in Camp
MINNESOTA—Giant of Mesabi
MISSISSIPPI—A Tradition of Pride
MISSOURI—Show Me

MONTANA—Big Sky Country
NEBRASKA—Boss Man from Ogallala
NEVADA—Reilly's Woman
NEW HAMPSHIRE—Heart of Stone
NEW JERSEY—One of the Boys
NEW MEXICO—Land of Enchantment
NEW YORK—Beware of the Stranger
NORTH CAROLINA—That Carolina Summer
NORTH DAKOTA—Lord of the High Lonesome
OHIO—The Widow and the Wastrel
OKLAHOMA—Six White Horses
OREGON—To Tell the Truth
PENNSYLVANIA—The Thawing of Mara
RHODE ISLAND—Strange Bedfellow
SOUTH CAROLINA—Low Country Liar
SOUTH DAKOTA—Dakota Dreamin'
TENNESSEE—Sentimental Journey
TEXAS—Savage Land
UTAH—A Land Called Deseret
VERMONT—Green Mountain Man
VIRGINIA—Tide Water Lover
WASHINGTON—For Mike's Sake
WEST VIRGINIA—Wild and Wonderful
WISCONSIN—With a Little Luck
WYOMING—Darling Jenny

THE HOMEPLACE

Harlequin Books

TORONTO • NEW YORK • LONDON
AMSTERDAM • PARIS • SYDNEY • HAMBURG
STOCKHOLM • ATHENS • TOKYO • MILAN

The state flower depicted on the cover of this book is wild
rose.

Janet Dailey Americana edition published January 1987
Second printing May 1988
Third printing June 1989
Fourth printing June 1990
Fifth printing August 1991

ISBN 0-373-21915-6

Harlequin Presents edition published October 1976
Second printing June 1979
Third printing February 1982

Original hardcover edition published in 1976
by Mills & Boon Limited

THE HOMEPLACE

CHAPTER ONE

THE BOYER RIVER WAS FROZEN OVER. A blanket of snow covered the pasture ground. Out of the leaden sky came more flakes gently drifting down like white flower petals on a spring day. The wind was still, although there was a nippiness in the air. Except for the crystalline flakes, the whole world seemed to have come to a standstill. Nothing moved, not even the girl standing so silently on the knoll above the river.

Her jade-green eyes surveyed the scene, nostalgia gripping her throat over all the bygone memories, but Catherine Carlsen refused to cry. She was taking a walk back into the past one last time and she didn't want tears blurring her vision.

Below her, where the river made its sweeping bend, was the place where the gentle rapids began, the place that, as a child, she had been allowed to swim. At the bottom of the hill where she was standing, the water was deeper. It was there that she and Clay used to fish for bullheads and catfish with their bamboo poles and a can of nightcrawlers unearthed behind the machine shed. Farther on was an island, barely discernible now from the ice-covered river, but that was where they had launched their home-made raft. They had watched their visions of reenacting the adventures of Huckleberry Finn sink with their raft.

The memories were endless. Each place her gaze rested brought more recollections of her childhood days. The lone willow tree lay horizontally, almost covered by the winter blanket. It looked bleak and lonely with its limbs sheared of summer foliage. The tiny spring-fed stream that the willow bridged wasn't visible under the snow, but many times she had quenched her thirst in its icy-cold waters in the height of a hot summer day.

Although the majority of her memories came from the summer seasons, Cathie recalled, too, the ice-skating on the river when the ice grew thick and firm and sledding down the hill toward the river, always stopping a hair's breadth short of its bank. Or the time the adults built a bonfire at the top of the hill so there would be a place to warm themselves in between trips down the hill on a sled or a shovel. Cathie remembered so well how she had sat with her feet close to the fire so she could warm her freezing toes. She had warmed them, but she had also melted the soles off her brand new rubber boots.

How often had she visualized the day when she would bring her own children out here and show them all the places she had played as a child? Now it was never to be. The land no longer belonged to the Carlsen family. The Homeplace, as it had been affectionately called, was no longer home. And she, Cathie Carlsen, was at that very moment a trespasser.

Something brushed the side of her leg. As she

turned her gaze down, Cathie's eyes met the earnest, imploring look of the English shepherd dog, Duchess. No matter what the circumstances there was always an apologetic look about the dog's face. The sad brown eyes were expressing their sorrow at intruding on Cathie's solitude even as Duchess inched closer for a reassuring caress of forgiveness. Obligingly Cathie removed a gloved hand from her pocket to fondle the red gold head.

"Hello, Duchess. What are you doing down here so far from the house?" Cathie noticed with sadness the collection of gray hairs around the pointed muzzle. Even Duchess was beginning to show her age, and it seemed like only yesterday that she had arrived on the farm, a frightened and bewildered puppy. "Did you get lonely up there, pretty lady?"

"She misses your grandfather."

Cathie turned toward the man standing a few paces behind her. "Hello, Clay," she said. "I didn't expect to see you here today."

Clay Carlsen studied her thoughtfully, choosing to ignore the vague ring of sarcasm in her low-pitched voice. He silently admired the way the brown fake fur coat enhanced the golden highlights of her honey-colored hair. The shoulder length cut curled beneath the strong line of her jaw and softened her high cheekbones. Yet her feminine features retained their look of strength and determination that was carried through so dominantly in her personality. The saving grace of her femininity was the vivid green of her eyes surrounded by thick dark lashes and the supremely sensuous line of her mouth. The vision of those lips, soft and yielding under the touch of his own, brought a smile to Clay's previously somber face.

"Like you, Cathie," he answered her quietly, "I thought I would make a sentimental journey over our old stamping grounds."

"Mother and Aunt Dana are up to the house packing the personal things that won't be put up for sale at the auction," she sighed, turning away from him to stare out over the river. "I'm supposed to be up there helping them sort through Grandpa and Grandma's things."

"It's a thankless job, but it has to be done."

"I know that." She flashed him a fiery look. Her yellow gold hair was a gift from the Scandinavian ancestors of her grandparents, but her mother's Irish side of the family received the credit for her jewel-colored eyes and the blame for her quick temper. Clay had never known quite how to handle that spitfire temper even when they were children. He was twenty-six, nearly three full years her senior, yet he had always been the one to bow to her wishes rather than bear the brunt of one of her rages. Normally Cathie was a loving, generous person, and that was the side of her that he adored. Over the years she had learned to control her temper, but it was those odd times when it sprang to the surface that Clay liked to avoid.

"I shouldn't have snapped at you like that, Clay," Cathie apologized, but her voice was tinged with the bitterness that had been building inside her. "I can't get used to losing Grandfather and the farm in less than two weeks."

"I know it's a terribly trite thing to say, but it's probably better that it happened this way," Clay said. He wished that Cathie would cry and release some of the grief she had kept bottled up.

"Why?" she demanded.

"First, because ever since your grandmother passed away last fall, your grandfather has been lost without her. And secondly, I think it was a good thing that the farm was sold almost the very day it was put on the market. It leaves no time for uncertainties and doubts. Often it's better that the separation is swift and sure. There's no time left for agonizing and brooding over the coming loss."

"We didn't have to lose it at all," Cathie retorted grimly. Her unseen hands were doubled into tight fists in her pockets.

"You didn't really expect your father to buy the farm, did you?"

"He could have." Her chin tilted upward as she cast him a defiant glance.

"Then what? Did you expect him to give up his professorship at the university? He isn't a young man any more. He couldn't have managed the farm by himself. Or would you have preferred him to lease it out as your grandfather did and have someone else farm it for him? With no one living in the house, it would have deteriorated in no time." There was an exasperated sound in Clay's voice. "Be sensible about this, Cathie."

"He could have bought it," she repeated. "And after you and I were married, we could have lived here and farmed it ourselves."

"I'm a lawyer, not a farmer," Clay stated emphatically. "I didn't spend all those years in college studying law to throw it aside because of some sentimental nonsense."

As soon as Clay had said it, he realized he had just waved a red cape in front of Cathie. Her reaction was instantaneous.

"It is *not* sentimental nonsense! And if you think it is, then I'm proud to be a sentimental fool! The very first plowshare that broke this ground when it was a wild prairie was held by my great-grandfather Carlsen. He was one of the first settlers in this area after the Civil War. Look at this land, Clay. It's one of the richest sections of bottom land in Iowa. The dirt is black and fertile, made to grow food and families. This is where our family began. This is the Carlsen home, our legacy given to us by our ancestors. Doesn't that mean anything to you?"

"Of course it does," he placated. "All of the family is sad to lose it, your father and myself included. But family farms are a passing thing. And you just can't live in the past anymore, not if you want to succeed in life. It's progress, Cathie."

"Then progress be damned!"

"Don't swear, Cathie. It isn't becoming," he admonished gently, all the while thinking what a bewitching creature she was when she was in a temper, her eyes flashing green fires and her face alive with passionate zeal.

"Why? Is swearing strictly a masculine right? Surely we've progressed to the point where a woman can swear if she wants to," she demanded sarcastically. "Sometimes I wish I were a man!"

"Well, I'm glad you're not. Otherwise you wouldn't be wearing my ring on your finger," Clay laughed, attempting to instill some lightness in the overcharged atmosphere. But Cathie deliberately ignored him.

"The thing that angers me most of all is that the farm is being sold to an outsider, to some imbecilic person from the east coast! He's probably some big business executive who's only interested in a tax deduction. He'll probably send some stupid manager out here to live on it while the farm falls to rack and ruin."

"You're being melodramatic. If he is a business man, and we know absolutely nothing about him, then he definitely will bring someone in who knows farming so he can get a return on his investment."

"Don't bet on it," she jeered.

"Why are you putting yourself through all this?" Clay sighed, taking her by the shoulders and turning her to face him, his hazel eyes taking in the belligerent and rebellious expression on her usually lovely face. "You can't change the fact that the farm is sold. It's useless to torment yourself with visions of what may or may not happen. Everything always works out for the best. This all was probably what was meant to happen."

"Fate, that's your answer for losing the Homeplace." A dullness clouded her eyes as her shoulders sagged beneath his hands. "You're probably right, but I'll never accept that it's for

the best. It just doesn't seem right that there
never will be a Carlsen living on this farm
again."

"Do you want to know something?" He lifted
her chin with his gloved finger. "You're usually
always so practical that it's rather nice to discover again how emotional you can get."

"How angry, you mean." A rueful smile
curved her lips. "But I never could stay mad at
you for very long, even when we were children."

"That's what made it so nice to be only kissing cousins." Clay Carlsen smiled. "It was
always so much fun to make up."

"Kissing cousins" had become a standard
joke between them since they had reached their
teens and were able to understand that even
though they shared the same last name of Carlsen, the actual blood relationship between them
was virtually nonexistent. Clay's great-grandfather had been a second cousin to Cathie's great-
grandfather. With that knowledge, Clay and
Cathie had progressed from childhood play-
mates to sweethearts and had reached the stage
of engagement.

"What's going to be done with Duchess?"
Clay asked as the dog whined to attract attention.

"I'm taking her to town with me," Cathie
answered, moving out of Clay's hold to kneel
beside the dog. "The Darbys offered to take her,
but she's getting so old that I think she would
have trouble adjusting to new people and a new
place, too."

"Do you think she's going to find it any easier

living in town? At least with the Darbys she would be on a farm and there would be someone around all the time. Whereas you'll be at school the biggest part of the day."

"We'll work it out, won't we, Duchess?" The aging shepherd wagged her tail enthusiastically in answer to the crooning voice, but Clay caught the disguised determination that plainly said Cathie intended to keep this last link with the farm.

"How much longer is Mrs. Carver staying on?" He conceded to her unspoken request to change the subject as he inquired about the housekeeper who had remained living in the farmhouse after Grandfather Carlsen's death.

"The real estate man asked her to stay on until a date has been set to turn the place over to the new owner," Cathie replied grimly, hating to acknowledge the existence of a new owner. "He didn't want the house to sit vacant."

"Which disproves your theory that the place was going to fall into rack and ruin."

"That was the real estate man's idea, so it proves absolutely nothing," she retorted sharply, rising to her feet, to the dog's disappointment. She looked out over the riverscape, shivering at the chilling reality of the situation.

"It's getting cold. Maybe it's time we were heading back to the house," Clay suggested. He pushed back the sleeve on his heavy corduroy parka to glance at his wristwatch. "Nearly four o'clock. That's later than I thought. I have a couple of stops to make. Which also reminds me, what time do you want me to pick you up tonight?"

"If you don't mind, I'll take a raincheck for tonight." Cathie accepted his guiding hand on her elbow that turned her in the direction of the house. "This is mother's last night. She's driving back to the university tomorrow afternoon, so I think I should spend the evening with her."

"No, I don't mind at all," he said as he helped her negotiate the barbed wire of the pasture fence while Duchess trotted to a small ditch and burrowed under the fence to keep up with them. "Are your parents driving back for the auction?"

"No," Cathie sighed. "And I can't say that I blame them. I don't think I will go either."

"It might be a good chance to pick up some furniture for our house," he ventured, unsure as to how far he should push the issue of forcing her to accept the sale.

"All the good furniture is antique and you know how these antique dealers drive up the prices at farm sales. We couldn't afford to pay that much plus the cost of storing until we find a decent house in our price range." Cathie shook her head with resigned sadness. "The family decided I could have the set of crystal in the way of a wedding present and a few other inexpensive mementoes. I'm satisfied with that."

The rutted pasture track had brought them to the farmyard. Cathie refused to let her gaze roam over the various buildings and once more fall in the grip of her many poignant memories. She kept walking toward the two-storey house with friendly gray smoke rising from its chimney to mingle with the scattering of snowflakes.

"Are you coming in? I'm sure Mrs. Carver would fix us some cocoa," she offered as they reached the green compact car that belonged to Clay.

"Not this time. I'll see you in church tomorrow, won't I?"

Cathie nodded and lifted her head for his goodbye kiss. He claimed her mouth with the gentleness and tenderness that was so much a part of his nature. Then Clay was climbing behind the wheel of his car. Cathie watched him as he drove out of the yard onto the county road that led to the highway before she turned toward the house, following the sidewalk through the metal gate to the back door of the white structure.

"I'm back," Cathie called out as she walked in the door and climbed the few steps of the inside landing to the sun porch. The snow-white hair atop Mrs. Carver's head caught her eye, drawing Cathie's attention to the kitchen. "Where are my mother and Aunt Dana?" she asked, traversing the narrow width of the sun porch to the large kitchen.

"They're in the back bedroom packing away Mr. Carlsen's clothes for the Salvation Army," the housekeeper replied, not pausing in her brisk stirring of some liquid in a bowl. The vigorous movement sent her rotund figure vibrating. A sharp eye was turned on Cathie. "Didn't you ask your young man to come in? I was just stirring up some frosting for a chocolate cake I made."

"Clay had some errands to run, so he couldn't stay."

"There you are, Catherine. I thought I heard your voice." Her mother stood in the kitchen doorway, her auburn hair glinting in the artificial light that couldn't detect a trace of gray. "Didn't Clay come in with you?"

Cathie repeated her previous statement to Mrs. Carver as she marveled again over her mother's youthful appearance even though she had passed the forty mark several years ago.

"That's too bad," Maureen Carlsen replied when she heard that Clay had left. "I was going to ask him to carry this box of clothes out to the station wagon. I'm afraid it's too big for Dana and me to carry. I suppose we could scoot it along the floor and down the steps."

Eyes that were nearly as green as Cathie's studied the route that the box would ultimately have to take before her mother nodded to herself that the plan would work. With that problem solved, she turned her attention back to her daughter.

"Well, did you and Clay tramp over all your playgrounds?" she asked with a bright and indulgent smile.

"More or less," Cathie shrugged, not wanting to discuss how unsatisfactory their conversation was. "What's left to be sorted?"

"Men are seldom as sentimental as we women are." Her mother astutely guessed the reason for her daughter's noncommittal reply. "Look at your father. He's so steeped in American literature that he can barely remember our anniversary. But I've learned to accept that the day of our marriage doesn't rank high compared to the early demise of Edgar Allan Poe."

"Dad isn't the least bit absentminded," Cathie protested with an amused smile. "He always remembers our birthdays and the holidays and he always picks out some wonderful, nonsensical gift for us. I don't believe he's ever forgotten your anniversary either."

"I would hope not! I feed him rice every single night for a week to be sure he gets the message," her mother laughed.

"This is a fine time for you to come back to the house, Cathie," her aunt Dana declared, coming to a halt behind her mother. "Just when we've packed the last box. You can take your coat off. You won't need to run back outside."

Long ago Cathie had learned that no matter how biting the comments of her father's older sister sounded, they were not meant that way. Dana Madison had simply never learned tact. With that knowledge, Cathie let the implied criticism slip by without comment.

"I suppose you also let Clay slip away without thinking to invite him in," Dana continued, taking the brown fur parka from Cathie's shoulders.

"He had some errands," Cathie repeated for the third time.

"Have you two set the wedding date yet?" her aunt asked crisply.

"Not yet."

"Ye gods, you two really believe in long engagements!" Dana exclaimed with scorn. "How long has it been since he gave you that ring?"

"Shortly after he passed his bar exam, which

was about a year ago," Cathie answered calmly, exchanging a silent look with her smiling mother.

"Let's see, the first excuse was that you were both in college and that it would be too great a strain financially for you to get married. Then it was that you wanted to find a teaching job." Dana was using her fingers to tick off the reasons why their marriage hadn't taken place. "After that, Clay had to pass his bar examination. At least you got an engagement ring then. What's your reason for waiting so long now?"

"We're trying to find a house. Neither one of us wants to live in an apartment even if there was a decent one available, which there isn't. So far we haven't been able to find a house in our price range that's fit to live in," Cathie attempted to explain logically their delay. "But in the meantime, we're saving our money so we can furnish the house when we do get it."

"In my day, we got married and moved in with our parents until we could afford something better."

"That wouldn't work for Clay and me since neither one of our parents live here any more. Besides, we're both enjoying our last bit of freedom without the responsibility of school and all."

"You make marriage sound like a prison," her aunt harumphed.

"There is a confining side to it," Cathie admitted.

"How old are you now? Twenty-three? Twenty-four?"

"I'll be twenty-four on my next birthday."

"And unmarried. That was practically a crime when I was young. We were considered almost old maids, weren't we, Maureen?" The older woman addressed her question to Cathie's mother.

"Customs have changed since then," her mother shrugged.

"I don't know if it's for the better," Dana sniffed indignantly. "In the past, the family home was passed from one generation to another but here we are selling the very place where we were born and raised. It's a shame that you and Dorian couldn't purchase it, Maureen. I wanted to put in a bid, but Al put his foot down, insisting that it just wasn't practical for us to buy it either."

"It is unfortunate that none of us was able to prevent the farm from going out of the family," Maureen Carlsen agreed with a note of sadness that was felt by all.

"Did you tell Cathie that the real estate agent called today?" Dana inquired.

"What about?" Cathie prompted, her honey-blond hair turning toward the older, graying woman.

"To let us know that the new owner will be taking possession, or wants to take possession, the fifteenth of March."

"So soon," Cathie murmured, a pallor stealing the color from her face. That was just over a week away.

"Yes. I guess it was a good thing we set the date for the auction as soon as we did," her aunt Dana nodded sagely. "The agent is making arrangements for Mrs. Carver to have some sleeping quarters for those few extra days between the auction and the new owner's arrival."

"What I'm hoping," Mrs. Carver inserted, bringing her newly frosted cake to the small dinette table in the kitchen, "is that the new owner will keep me on. I just have too much time on my hands to set at home alone. Goodness knows there isn't much call for housekeepers anymore, not around here anyway. Did that real estate man find out anything about the new owner, Mrs. Madison?"

"From what I could gather," Dana replied in her caustic voice, "all he knows is that the man's name is Robert Douglas and he lives in Long Island, New York. The agent never asked if the man was married or single, young or old, whether he intended to farm it himself or hire someone else. I suppose all the agent cares about is his commission."

"It seems to me that a man who would buy a piece of property sight unseen isn't the type who would make it his home," Cathie stated bitterly.

"Now, I heard that the man flew up here in a private plane the day the real estate man contacted him," Mrs. Carver said, drawing the immediate attention of the rest of the group.

"Did you see him?" Cathie's mother asked, voicing the question that rose in all three minds.

"No." The housekeeper shook her head. "If he actually came out to the farm, he never came to the house."

"That's the first I've heard of any visit," Dana

commented, plainly showing her dislike of receiving that piece of information so late. "Who told you that?"

"One of the men from the real estate office when he came out to make a list of the equipment that was sold with the land," Mrs. Carver replied. "Of course, it might not have been the same man that bought the farm, but that's the way I understood him." The cake knife expertly slashed through the white frosting. "Now all of you have to have a piece of this cake before you leave."

CHAPTER TWO

THE SCHOOL CLASSROOM was abnormally quiet.
The rows of desks were empty of children except
for one boy studiously crouched over his paper.
Behind the large desk next to the blackboard,
Cathie Carlsen was correcting the last of the
fourth grade arithmetic papers. Her blond hair
was pulled away from her face and secured at
the nape of her neck by a scarf that matched the
peacock-blue and jade-green paisley print of her
silk blouse. As she placed the last paper on top
of the neat stack, Cathie glanced at the large
wall clock. Rising quietly from her desk, she
walked down the row of desks to where the
nine-year-old was sitting. Over his shoulder she
read the scrawling words 'I will not glue books
together' repeated over and over again. The boy
turned his freckled face toward her, his sandy-
brown hair sticking out in all directions, the
result of innumerable cowlicks that laughed at
combs and brushes.

"Can I go home now, Miss Carlsen?" he
pleaded, his sparkling brown eyes using their
influence to the fullest.

"May I go home," Cathie corrected.

"May I go home?" he sighed, his shoulders
slumping at the lack of response to his beguiling
look.

Charles Smith, or as he was known to his classmates Charlie, was the instigator of nearly every misdeed done during the course of a school day. Behind the bewitching innocence of his freckled face was a midget monster who was either in mischief or thinking of it. Today's escapade had involved gluing Mary Tate's schoolbooks together during the lunch period. Mary, who possessed a desire for learning, was one of the more intelligent pupils in Cathie's class, which earned Mary the nickname of "teacher's pet" and the revenge of Charlie for her almost perfect behavior.

"Yes, you may go home now, Charlie." Her acquiescence was followed by slamming books and shuffling papers as Charlie raced to accomplish his escape before Cathie could change her mind and make him stay longer. He was halfway to the coatroom when she called her warning after him. "The next time you get into trouble, you'll go straight to the principal's office."

"There won't be a next time, Miss Carlsen," he assured her, backing slowly but surely toward his coat.

"I hope not."

It was difficult keeping a severe expression on her face. She had long ago resigned herself to the fact that every class had a Charlie Smith. And as long as they kept to the frogs and the spitballs and avoided the destructive mischief, the best course was to mark it up to the exuberance of youth, and especially small boys with their snips and snails and puppy dogs' tails.

A few minutes later Cathie was slipping on her three-quarter-length black leather coat and picking up the case filled with her own "homework" to follow Charlie Smith's path out of the brick schoolhouse. The house that she shared with two girl friends was conveniently only three blocks from the school, thus eliminating the expense of driving her car back and forth. On blustery days like today, the three blocks were just about all that Cathie wanted to walk.

Two weeks had passed since her visit to the farm. The auction had taken place and presumably the new owner had moved in, since the possession date had gone by. Still, in this the latter part of March, there remained a trace of snow on the ground and March promised to go out like a lion instead of a lamb. Spring was several corners away.

Duchess, the English shepherd, was huddled next to her new kennel. At the sight of Cathie walking up the sidewalk, she rose to a crouching sit, her tail tucked between her legs and her head lowered near to the ground as if the chain attached to her collar weighed too heavily on her neck. The forlornly sad eyes watched Cathie's approach.

"How was your day, Duchess?" Cathie asked brightly, trying to ignore the woebegone expression on the dog's face but not succeeding. "I'm sorry I have to tie you up, pretty lady, but you keep running away if I don't."

There was the teeniest wagging of the feathery red, gold and white tail at the soothing sound of Cathie's voice. As the chain hook was unsnapped the wagging increased, although Duchess remained subdued, attaching herself to Cathie's heels to follow her inside the house. There, the shepherd went immediately to the hallway rug where she could keep an eye on all of the comings and goings of the household occupants and especially her beloved new mistress.

Neither of Cathie's two roommates were home yet. Connie Murchison worked in the local bank while Andrea, "Andy", Parker was a dental assistant. Since Cathie was usually always the first one home, she prepared their evening meal during the week and the other girls took the responsibility during the weekends. She was in the middle of mixing a meat loaf when Andy burst through the door.

"Oh, there you are, Cathie!" she cried exuberantly, her cap of dark hair ruffled by the brisk wind outside. "You'll never guess who I met today!" In the midst of taking off her brown corduroy parka, she glanced over Cathie's shoulder. "What's for supper tonight? Ummm, meat loaf. Baked potatoes, too? Oh, with gobs of butter and sour cream," Andy groaned. "And just imagine all the calories! Not everybody is like you, Cathie, and can eat anything they want and not gain an ounce of weight."

"You could eat the baked potato with butter and not sour cream or vice versa," Cathie laughed. Andy was on a perpetual diet in a losing battle to combat her tendency toward overweight.

"I could," Andy agreed, lifting her shoulders in a characteristic acceptance of fate, "but potatoes taste so much better with both."

"What are you doing home so early? It isn't even five o'clock."

"Dr. Roland had a meeting of some kind, so he decided to close the office early. That reminds me, I started to tell you who I met today and we got sidetracked." Enthusiasm once more bubbled to the surface as Andy flung her coat on the chair and danced back to the sink to clean the potatoes for Cathie. "Dr. Roland sent me to the bank to make the deposit after work. When I walked into the bank I saw Connie talking to this gorgeous hunk of man. Naturally I went over there to say hello. You could tell she was absolutely furious with me, but she had to introduce me to him just the same. As luck would have it, the very second after she'd introduced us, old Mr. Hammer wanted to see Connie and I was left alone with him."

"Left alone with whom, Andy?" Amused exasperation curved Cathie's lips at her girl friend's uncanny ability to drag out explanations.

"With Robert Douglas." The way Andy made the pronouncement, Cathie expected a trumpet fanfare to blare from some hidden speaker in the room. During the brief span of seconds before Andy continued her recounting of her meeting, Cathie tried to place where she had heard the name before. "You know," Andy prompted at the blank look she was receiving, "the man who bought your grandparents' farm."

There was an instantaneous rise of antagonism inside Cathie. She had to halt her molding of the meat into a loaf for fear she would mash it into a pie. But Andy didn't pay any attention to the adverse reaction she had received, logically thinking that Cathie would be interested to hear about the new owner.

"He is a dream! He's tall, over six foot, and lean. He's got thick, wavy brown hair, the kind that you want to run your fingers through, and beautiful brown eyes that just make you melt when you look at him. And talk about a tan! He made everybody look as if they'd been hibernating. Oh, and he was wearing this cashmere sweater that was out of this world. So was the physique it covered! My guess is that he's about thirty something, thirty-two or three probably. Another neat thing about him was his voice. It was low-pitched and quiet as if what he was saying was only meant for you to hear. I mean, it was really sexy."

"Are you sure you didn't forget something?" Cathie asked caustically, irritated by her friend's enthusiasm for this usurper of her family home.

"Yes!" Andy exclaimed with a gasp, as if she had forgotten the most important thing. "He had a scar. A little inch-long scar near the corner of his . . . right eye. It makes him look sort of—" a dreamy expression crept into Andy's eyes "—rugged and masculine."

The oven door banged loudly shut after Cathie jammed in the meat loaf pan.

Andy handed her the potatoes neatly wrapped in aluminium foil. "Here, you can put these in the oven, too. Do you want to know something else I found out about him that's just absolutely rotten?"

Visions of bulldozers tearing down the farmhouse to make room for an ultramodern ranch
home sprang immediately to mind. "What?"
Cathie breathed, half afraid to hear the answer.

Andy sighed heavily, "He's married. The first
really neat guy that moves into the area has to
be married. Is that some kind of luck!"

The muscles that had tensed in anticipation of
some shocking news relaxed and Cathie laughed
in relief. "You didn't just come right out and ask
him that, did you?"

A suitably injured expression appeared on the
dark-haired girl's face. "I'm not totally lacking
in tact, Cathie. Besides—" an impish grin spread
over her face "—he had a little boy with him
who kept calling him father. I just reasoned it
out that where there was a daddy and a little
boy, there had to be a mommy."

"That wouldn't necessarily follow. He could
be divorced or a widower." Now why had she
said that, Cathie wondered to herself.

"Wouldn't that be wonderful if he was
eligible!" Andy clasped her hands together in
glee. "Not that it would bother Connie if he was
married or not. She's terribly unscrupulous
when it comes to good-looking men, and Rob
Douglas was one handsome male! Which
reminds me, you'll probably meet him yourself.
He's enrolling his boy in school here. Naturally
I mentioned that my roommate, meaning you,
was a teacher and also the granddaughter of the
former owners of his farm."

"What grade is his boy in?" A terrible feeling
of dread encompassed her as Cathie wondered if

she could be objective about a pupil being the son of the man whom she already resented for buying the family farm.

A frown creased Andy's forehead. "I don't think he said. I remember telling him that you taught the fourth grade, but I can't recall that he made any comment, and I'm such a lousy judge of ages I couldn't tell you whether the boy was seven or eleven. I imagine you'll find out soon enough." She shrugged, not attaching any major importance to the subject. "What's on your agenda for this evening? Are you and Clay going somewhere?"

"I have choir practice at the church. Clay's meeting me afterward, but just for coffee, nothing special."

"That sounds more exciting than my plans for this evening. I'm going to wash my hair, rinse out a few sweaters and watch the late show. You don't realize how lucky you are, Cathie," the other girl accused, wallowing unashamedly in self-pity. "First of all, you have a steady guy, which is a major achievement in itself, and secondly, he's one terrific feller. If I were you, I'd have him walking to that altar so fast that he wouldn't know what had happened. And I sure wouldn't let him anywhere near Connie. She goes after anything in pants. Don't you ever get jealous when she flirts with Clay right in front of you? I almost want to scratch her eyes out for you."

"Jealousy just isn't a part of my nature, I guess." Cathie lifted her shoulders expressively. "Either that or it's just that I trust Clay."

A thoughtful gleam glittered as Andy eyed the blonde busily setting the small dinette table. "Why haven't you two set your wedding date yet?"

"No particular reason." Jade-green eyes raised their gaze to meet the pair of curious brown ones. "We've been looking for a house and have more or less postponed setting a date until we find one."

"Doesn't Clay object? I mean, does he really want to wait?"

The question caught Cathie off guard. Had Clay ever voiced an opinion in the matter? She couldn't recall that he had. He had simply always agreed to whatever she suggested. Andy was waiting for an answer.

"It was just something we mutually agreed on," Cathie replied calmly, not letting the sudden flickering of doubt be revealed.

"Don't you love him?" At the startled expression on Cathie's face, Andy hurried on with a further explanation. "I always imagined that when you love someone, really love them, it just sweeps you away in a tide of passion. Yet you sound so coldly practical about it sometimes, unless you . . . ." A shy flush of color filled Andy's cheeks as she hesitated before completing her sentence. "Unless you and Clay . . . I mean, a lot of engaged couples don't wait for the actual ceremony. I know it's none of my business, but I just wondered if you were 'saving yourself,' so to speak, for your wedding night."

"Andy, you are priceless!" Cathie couldn't keep the bubbling sound of amusement out of her voice. "Saving yourself! What a beautifully old-fashioned expression! But I guess that's exactly what I have been doing. For me, it's always been Clay. I knew I was going to marry him when I was in the eighth grade, and he's such a perfect gentleman, that I don't think it would occur to him to suggest anything different except to wait until we're married. We were both raised with what many people would consider old-fashioned morals. And as for getting swept off my feet by a man on a white horse—" a grin teased the corners of her mouth "—I could never picture Clay that way. I would always remember that Hallowe'en costume he wore one year when we were children. It was a cowboy suit and he had his two front teeth missing. It's not an image that fits well with a knight in shining armor."

"It would 'tarnish' it," Andy declared, laughing at her own pun. "Not that I would know since I never had a childhood sweetheart or a girlhood sweetheart or any sweetheart for that matter. The plain fact is I talk too much and no matter what I do I can't seem to keep my mouth shut. And you know how men are. They prefer listeners so they can talk about themselves."

"Listening isn't so hard to learn."

"As long as the person doing the talking is saying something interesting." Andy headed for the hallway, but paused in its doorway. "I've always had this fantasy that some day the right guy would come along and kiss me just to shut me up. And his kisses would be so terrific that they would rob me of all speech. That's silly,

isn't it?" she sighed, "but I was just born romantic. Which is probably why you're going to
marry your comfortable and ever-present Clay
and why I don't have a date for Saturday
night!"

Andy's thought-provoking comments remained even after she had gone into her own small
bedroom to change out of her white uniform.
With dinner in the oven and the timer set,
Cathie filled the bathtub and let the bubbly,
scented water soak away the day's tensions
while her mind kept wandering back to Andy's
conversation. There had been the underlying
impression that Andy thought Cathie was settling for second best, which was absurd, because
she loved Clay. Admittedly there wasn't the
white-hot, searing flame of passion between
them that Andy placed so much importance on,
but Cathie considered that an overrated com-
modity. It wasn't nearly as important as respect
and friendship and undemanding affection.

From some unbidden corner of her mind
came the thought that it would be nice to feel all
of those and an unquenchable desire, too. With
a sharp shake of her head, Cathie dismissed it.

"Fairy-tale stuff," she murmured to the open-
mouthed ceramic fish on the bathroom wall.
Fictional accounts of love had never borne any
resemblance to reality in Cathie's sphere of
knowledge.

Although she had been positive that she
would marry Clay, that hadn't stopped her from
dating other men when she was in high school
and college. Therefore she had more than her

experience with Clay to draw on. Kissing had always been a pleasant experience and some men had more finesse than others, but there had never been any throbbing, heat-filled kisses to carry her off to any dizzy heights of desire. Any accounts of such happenings Cathie had always marked off as poetic licence.

Besides, what did it matter to her if Andy didn't find her relationship with Clay particularly romantic, Cathie thought as she briskly rubbed herself dry with the big bath towel. She was very contented with Clay. From a distant part of her mind, she heard Andy's voice mocking her, "Like a cow chewing its cud?"

Cathie gave herself a mental shake. It was foolish to be suddenly questioning her decision to marry Clay or her own views about love and what it meant. They were beliefs she had held for years and simply because they differed from those of someone else that was not a reason for her to doubt their validity.

Slipping the black sweater vest that matched the yellow and black plaid slacks over her white blouse, Cathie removed the confining hairband from her head. The oven timer would be buzzing any minute now, so she postponed putting on her makeup until after the meal, pausing only long enough to run a brush through her hair.

Andy was sitting in the middle of the living room floor, painstakingly attempting to roll her short hair around pink plastic rollers.

"Why is it—" Andy groaned at the sight of Cathie "—that if brunettes are supposed to have thick, full-bodied hair, I have this thin, fine stuff and you, a blonde, have the thick gorgeous hair?" Her shoulders slumped as a lock of hair slipped out of her grasp. "I have to use a ton of this setting gel to persuade this darn hair to look at a roller!"

A statuesque girl appeared in the doorway, her cool gray eyes surveying the scene with superiority. "Have you ever considered a perm, Andrea?" Long hair that was an unusual combination of brown streaked with blond was swung over her shoulder in a graceful gesture as Connie Murchison entered the room.

"And end up with the frizzies! Not on your life!" Andy declared.

"Hello, Connie," Cathie greeted her second roommate. "Dinner will be ready shortly. How was your day?"

Connie tightened the sash on her ivory, floor-length silk robe before reclining her lanky form on the cinnamon couch. On cue the robe flicked open from the knee down to reveal her shapely legs and the lacy edge of her slip. "It had its moments," she smiled mysteriously.

"Cathie, you're psychic!" Andy exclaimed suddenly. "Do you remember when you said that just because Mr. Douglas had a little boy it didn't mean he was married? Well, you were right. Connie was just telling me that his wife died last fall. Isn't that tragic? I imagine that's why he moved out here, to get away from all the familiar things and start a new life."

"It didn't appear to me that his wife's death had left him all that choked up," Connie observed, lighting a cigarette and exhaling the smoke so that it drifted like a cloud in front of her face and hid the knowing gleam in her pale gray eyes.

"How would you know whether a man was in mourning or not," the dark-haired girl demanded. "Just because he wasn't wearing a black armband or grieving visibly over his loss it doesn't mean he didn't care about her dying."

"I just can't visualize a man who, according to you, is supposed to feel this intense loss for his 'beloved' wife accepting an invitation to a party," Connie replied calmly.

"A party!" Andy gasped in horror, bringing an amused smile to Cathie's face. Poor romantic Andy, she thought, was no match for Connie who launched her siege of an eligible male with the precision and expertise of an army general. "You haven't invited him to a party already! Why, you only met him today!" Andy finished.

"I wasn't about to let someone else snatch him up." A dark eyebrow lifted in mock surprise as if such an action would be traitorous to her nature, which it would. "As I told Rob, it's a small party and it will serve to get him acquainted with the local people."

"I think you're disgusting!" Andy declared, never one to hide her feelings.

"Why?" Connie shrugged. "He's a man who knows the score. I didn't suggest anything that he didn't want me to."

"Andy told me he was quite handsome." A spurt of cold anger drove Cathie to take part in the conversation.

A secret smile played around the corners of

Connie's mouth. "I assure you, whatever he is, he isn't a farmer. And if he ever had a little black book of telephone numbers, I'm positive it was filled."

"Why did he come out here, then? Why did he buy the farm?" Cathie demanded, unconscious that her hands were clenched tightly at her side.

"Really, Cathie!" A husky laugh sounded from the couch. "I haven't got to the point yet where Rob has confided everything to me. I know he has a very healthy bank balance. Maybe it's like Andy said. He's tired of being a playboy and wants to turn over a new leaf."

"Playboys aren't married men," Andy corrected sarcastically.

"You're such a naive child." Connie flashed the girl on the floor a saccharine-sweet smile.

The humming buzz of the oven timer acted as a deterrent to further conversation among the trio. Cathie pivoted around sharply to respond to it as Andie hopped to her feet to help.

"I don't think I'm going to like this Mr. Rob Douglas," Cathie muttered. Connie's description had left a bad taste in her mouth for the new owner of the Carlsen farm.

"You haven't even met the man." Andy turned a questioning look on her. "You aren't going to let Connie's assessment of him influence you? I thought he was a very charming and friendly man, but I certainly didn't get the lady-killing impression that she did."

Cathie paused in front of the oven door, a potholder in each hand, and glanced over her shoulder at Andy. "I'm not taking sides for or against the man," she said, forcing her temper to recede. "He means absolutely nothing to me and isn't likely to either."

CHAPTER THREE

THE FOLLOWING MORNING Mr. Graham, the principal, brought Cathie's new pupil to her classroom. Judging by the sullen expression on the boy's face, Tad Douglas was not any happier with the situation than Cathie was, although she was determined to make the best of it and not let her resentment of his father color her relationship with his son. In a silent admission to herself Cathie realized that it might prove difficult.

Tad Douglas had all the earmarks of a young boy who had been spoiled, his every whim indulged by a doting parent. His hazel eyes seemed to possess only two expressions; one was sullen and the other defiant. The impression he created with the rest of the class wasn't very good either. His sandy-brown hair was longer than that of the other members. His precisely creased slacks and crisply starched shirt didn't bear any resemblance to the casual shirts and denim jeans of the other boys. Cathie noticed the uneasy fidgeting in their seats as she introduced Tad to the rest of the class.

Charlie Smith didn't help. From his coveted back-row seat, she heard him snickering. "Tad, ain't that name short for tadpole?"

The boy sitting across the aisle whispered

back, "Tad is a frog!" More giggles followed from behind hand-covered mouths.

The invisible shell around Tad grew harder. His superior standoffish attitude during the rest of the school day did little to help him make friends. In Cathie's brief tenure as an elementary teacher she had learned there was no way that she could make his incorporation into the class any easier. It was up to Tad and the rest of the class, and neither was eager to take the first step.

While Cathie felt sorry for the newcomer's isolation imposed partly by the rest of the class, she was angered by his apathy. Not once during the entire day did he smile or show any interest in the lessons or the activities. Tad was the last one to leave the room during recess periods and the last one to return when they were over. He wasn't allowing any opportunity for anyone to make an overture of friendliness. There was something in his childish version of arrogance that said it had nothing to do with shyness. Tad Douglas simply did not want to make friends.

When class was dismissed at the end of the day, Tad made a project of slowly stacking his books while the rest of the students made their usual mad dash for the door. The room was cleared by the time Tad was done and ready to put on his own coat. Cathie felt compelled to show some interest in his welfare.

"Will your father be meeting you?" she inquired, forcing a smile to appear on her face.

"No," Tad shrugged, slipping his arms into the tailored overcoat. "He doesn't want to be bothered with me."

Cathie's ire at his unknown father increased, but she concealed it with the utmost difficulty. "I thought since it was your first day at school he might," she said calmly. "Do you know which school bus to take to get home?"

"Yes."

A glumly resigned look flitted across his face to tug at Cathie's heartstrings. If it hadn't been for the fact that walking with him to the school bus would have further alienated him from the rest of the class, Cathie would have done it. As it was she could only nod and add a cheerful, "See you tomorrow, Tad," a statement that earned her another sullen glance.

April and May were two very long months, especially for Tad Douglas and Cathie Carlsen. He proved to be a conscientious, intelligent student, his homework always turned in on time and usually always correct, but he never took part in any discussions or showed a desire to do so. Except on rainy days, the recess periods were held outside, with Tad remaining apart from the rest of the class unless there were organized games.

More than once Cathie had heard the chanting, "Tad is a frog! Tad is a frog!" and wondered at the unknowing cruelty of children.

Tad still lingered an extra few minutes at the end of the day. Cathie was never sure if he did it to avoid the ridicule of the children or if he attached importance to their brief exchanges.

One day she had asked him how he liked his new home. His small shoulders had made their habitual shrug beneath his expensive cotton shirt. "It's all right."

The lack of enthusiasm in his reply had caused her to add, "When I was a little girl about your age, I used to spend all my summers and most of my holidays on the very farm where you live."

She had expected some gleam of interest, but Tad had merely cast her a blank look and asked, "Why?" as if the farm was the last place in the world anyone would want to be.

"My grandparents lived there. I liked visiting them," Cathie continued determinedly, "and because there were so many fun places to play."

He had given her another look that plainly said she was out of her mind as he ended their conversation with, "I have to catch the bus."

Outside school, Cathie had only seen Tad once. That had been after a Sunday church service. She had changed out of her choir robe and was walking to the car park to meet Clay. Dressed in a blue suit and a striped tie, Tad was leaning against the fender of a shiny El Dorado. A toe of one polished shoe was digging furrows in the gravel.

He looked up at the sound of her approach. "Good morning, Miss Carlsen," Tad had greeted her politely.

"Good morning, Tad," Cathie returned. "I didn't know you attended this church." Her seat in the choir didn't give her much of a view of the congregation, so it didn't surprise her that she hadn't seen him.

"It was my father's idea," he said, indicating that the thought was definitely not his. "I did see you in the choir, though."

"Next time I'll look for you," Cathie smiled, glancing around her. "Where's your father?"

"Ah, he's talking to somebody." Tad sighed with the impatience of youth.

At that moment Clay had joined them. "There you are, Cathie. I've been looking for you."

"I stopped to talk to Tad. Clay, this is one of my students, Tad Douglas," Cathie introduced. "This is Clay Carlsen."

"Is he your husband?" Tad looked Clay over with almost grown-up speculation.

"No, he's my fiancé." To which the boy nodded with an indifferent understanding.

"Are you ready to go?" Clay asked as Tad turned his gaze away from them. Cathie had the feeling that Clay's arrival was the reason for Tad's unspoken wish to discontinue their conversation. She had told him goodbye and received a mumbled response.

"So that's your difficult pupil and the son of Rob Douglas," Clay remarked as they reached his car.

"Tad's not difficult," Cathie defended. "He just doesn't seem to be coping with his new environment."

"Why don't you discuss it with his father?" Clay suggested practically, opening the car door and helping Cathie inside.

Cathie took her time before replying, smoothing the accordion pleats of her yellow-flowered spring dress while Clay walked around to the driver's side and slid behind the wheel. She didn't want to get into a discussion with Clay about Rob Douglas. She knew he would scoff at the dread she felt at the thought of meeting Tad's father. Thus far Cathie hadn't seen him or spoken to him and she considered herself lucky that she hadn't. The opportunities had been there to do so. Her roommate, Connie, had had several dates with him, although none recently. Fortunately, as far as Cathie was concerned, Connie had always been ready the moment Rob Douglas had arrived. Andy attributed that to the fact that Connie wasn't eager to introduce him to any other female. Still, on those evenings when Rob Douglas had been expected, Cathie had kept to her room, using the pretext of school papers to correct.

The very fact that their eventual meeting had been prolonged added to its importance and to Cathie's apprehensions. Rob Douglas was firmly established as the new owner of the Carlsen farm, a circumstance that the passage of time hadn't been able to dampen her resentment about. And his son Tad's vague comments about him had tended to increase her antagonism. Most of all there was her own presentiment that once she met him there would be more catastrophic changes in her life beyond the loss of a piece of land that had been in her family for generations.

All of these feelings she had tried at one time or another to explain to Clay. He hadn't been able to understand or attach any importance to them and their discussions had always ended with Cathie losing her temper. Therefore, when Clay had suggested that she discuss Tad's adjustment to his new life with his father, she had passed it off with, "Tad will adjust in time after the newness wears off," and Clay had been content to accept that.

Like many of the other teachers, Cathie applauded the cries of "School's out! School's out! Teacher's let the monkeys out!" that heralded the beginning of summer vacation.

The increased workload of preparing final exams, grading them and filling out report cards convinced Cathie that the summer vacation was really for the teachers. There was pride in passing all her students on to the fifth grade and pity for Mrs. Gleason, who would inherit Charlie Smith with the rest of the class. Charlie had very considerately brought his pet garter snake to the class picnic, to the horror of the shrieking girls and the amusement of the laughing boys—all except Tad, who maintained his lonely onlooking position to the very end.

The week after school closed Cathie used to recuperate from her previous hectic pace. Although officially it was still spring, the weather had summer's heat. The first few mornings she slept late and lazed in the backyard, sunning herself to acquire the golden tan that came so naturally to her complexion. Then she indulged in a brief buying spree so her summer wardrobe would contain some of the newer fashions. It was difficult to keep from remembering that last year at this time she had spent her days at the Homeplace doing some of the heavier housework that her grandmother wasn't able to do anymore and indulging in her grandfather's passion for cribbage.

The rising sun cast a cherry-red glow over the horizon before climbing higher to shine in a cloudless blue sky. In the distance the pealing of bells chimed their announcement of Sunday's services. Her hair had a rich golden sheen as Cathie smoothed the white satin collar over her navy blue choir robe. Then she filed in with the rest of the choir to take her seat. The resonant sound of the organ filled the church as it began the prelude. The congregation stood to raise its voice to sing the hymn "Holy, Holy, Holy" and Cathie's alto voice joined in the harmony.

After resuming her seat, Cathie allowed her gaze to shift over the congregation. Her view was limited, but her eyes casually inspected those within her sight. A tiny smile curved her full lips as she spied the small, smartly dressed boy sitting erectly in the fourth pew. Tad's hazel eyes were scanning the choir, finally coming to rest on Cathie. Even at that distance, Cathie could see the slight nod of recognition he gave her. She did the same in return, her heart swelling with tenderness that this serious little boy wanted to exchange a secret greeting with her. Perhaps she had made some headway with him after all.

"The Scripture reading for this Sunday is Matthew 13:44," the Reverend Mr. Wittman intoned. " 'This kingdom of heaven is like treasure hidden in a field, which a man found and covered up; then in his joy he goes and sells all that he has and buys that field.' "

While Mr. Wittman was speaking, a movement beside Tad attracted Cathie's gaze. As she disengaged herself from Tad's look, she mentally braced herself for her first glimpse of Rob Douglas. Her heartbeat quickened.

His strong, powerful face blocked out all thought of her surroundings as she studied it. His hair was brown as Andy had said, but it was a rich, vibrant shade. Its thickness and wave defied any orderly style, but its casual, almost wayward appearance made the man all the more attractive. Still, it was his face that commanded Cathie's attention. It was lean, with a sharply defined mouth and artfully chiseled nose accented by a strong jaw line and firm chin. Dark brows curved above eyes that appeared dark, although at this distance Cathie had to assume his eyes were brown, and above the brows was a wide, intelligent forehead. There was nothing soft about Rob Douglas's face, but there was nothing harsh either.

Yet all the innuendoes, the implied but never spoken comments were stamped in his face and in the arrogant tilt of his head. He reeked of virile masculinity, the supreme dominating male— the type that liberated Cathie had always loathed. She was further irritated by the fact that all around him people were sitting so stiffly, obviously uncomfortable in their unaccustomed Sunday finery, while Rob Douglas sat relaxed and assured in his impeccably tailored brown suit.

Cathie saw him glance down at his son, then follow his gaze to the choir. Antagonism welled inside her as Rob Douglas met her gaze. She felt a flush of anger fill her cheeks at the suggestion

of amusement in his glance. Determinedly
Cathie turned her attention to the minister,
although through the rest of their service she
found her attention pulled back to Tad's father
as if he had some magnetic attraction.

The benediction signaled the close of the service. Cathie's movements were more hurried
than the rest of the choir as she hastened to
remove her robe and place it on its hanger.
There was no pause to brush her hair or retouch
her makeup. She simply adjusted the locket
around her neck, smoothing the bodice of her
pink dotted-swiss dress before gathering her
white leather handbag and slipping out through
the side door of the church. Escape seemed
mandatory and Cathie glanced furtively around
for Clay, only to see him cornered by Agnes
Rogers. Her white dress heels tapped the pavement impatiently as she debated whether to
walk over to free him from the woman's gossip-
ing tongue or to retreat to the car and let him
make his own excuses.

Before she could make a decision on the best
course of action, Cathie saw Tad approaching.
Something in the determination of his carriage
with its squared shoulders and erectly held head
told her that the only reason he was coming this
way was to see her. Cathie felt guilty for not
really wanting to see or talk to Tad at this
moment, but the antagonistic sensation she had
experienced toward his father was still too
strong for her to conduct herself naturally with
Tad, his son. As she debated turning away, pre-
tending she hadn't seen Tad, the opportunity to
do so evaporated.

The boy stopped stiffly in front of her and without any prelude of greetings said, "Miss Carlsen, my father would like to meet you, please."

If only the request had been made less formally, Cathie thought ruefully. A "Hey, my dad wants to meet you" would have put her so much more at ease.

The words of polite refusal formed. "My fiancé and I were just leaving. Perhaps—" Cathie almost said "another time" when she saw a look pass fleeting through his eyes that pleaded with her to consent. It was so unexpected to see an emotional reaction from Tad that Cathie immediately reformulated her reply for the boy's sake. "Perhaps since Clay is still talking to Mrs. Rogers, I'll have time to meet your father."

"He's over this way," Tad said, reaching to take her hand.

Silently chiding herself for falling victim to the beguiling boy, Cathie followed him through the thinning throng of churchgoers. Rob Douglas was talking to the minister when he spied them approaching. The lordly nod of goodbye that he gave Mr. Wittman as he turned to meet them set Cathie's teeth on edge. It was going to be difficult controlling her temper and maintaining the outward serenity a teacher is supposed to cultivate, Cathie realized.

He had an easy, graceful stride that covered ground quickly without appearing to do so. Now, at closer quarters, Cathie felt the full force of his attractiveness directed at her, the vitality and charm reaching out to pull her into his circle of admirers. Her eyes glittered with emerald green sparks as she resolved that she would not fall victim to the charisma that emanated from him. Let him find out that there were some women in this world who wouldn't hang on his every word, she thought with spiteful amusement.

The atmosphere between them was definitely charged as his velvet-brown eyes acknowledged the challenge in hers. Instead of being put off by it, Rob Douglas seemed to accept it and even find humor in it, which did little to smooth Cathie's already ruffled fur.

"This is my teacher, Miss Carlsen." Tad was taking his duties as introducer seriously. "Miss Carlsen, this is my father, Robert Douglas."

"How do you do, Mr. Dougals." The formal situation seemed to demand that there be a handshake, and very unwillingly Cathie offered hers.

"I'm very glad to meet you, Miss Carlsen." His mouth quirked with amusement as she practically snatched her hand away after only the briefest of contact with his. His voice was very clear and articulate but low-pitched, which Cathie decided was the reason Andy had described it as sexy, although she would only concede that it was pleasing to the ear. "My son has mentioned you many times. I believe he's sorry you won't be teaching him next year."

"Tad is a very good student." It was disconcerting to be at the disadvantage of having to look up because of the man's superior height.

Cathie welcomed the opportunity to direct her gaze elsewhere, this time at the young boy standing beside them. "I was happy to have him in my class."

"I believe you're right, Tad. Miss Carlsen does resemble Patience."

The unexpected remark brought her head up sharply. A quizzical look was in her eyes as she brushed a gold lock from her cheek.

"Patience is a little yellow kitten. She has honey-colored fur and green flashing eyes," Rob Douglas explained. The gaze that roamed over her face and hair left her with the peculiar feeling that he had touched her. It was a distinctly unsettling sensation.

"I see," Cathie breathed, turning away from the mesmerizing depths of the brown eyes in favor of the more innocuous hazel ones. "Is Patience one of your pets, Tad?"

"You can hardly get close to her unless you wait long enough. That's why we called her Patience." Tad tilted his head way back to look up at his father. "The other day she let me pet her. She even purred."

"Maybe it's just grown-ups she doesn't like," his father commented. Deep grooves were carved on each side of his mouth as he studied Cathie with open amusement. "Your name is Catherine, isn't it? Mr. Wittman told me. Do your friends call you Cat?"

"My friends call me Cathie, *Mr.* Douglas," she retorted sharply, her hold on her temper snapping at his implication.

"Your teacher has claws, Tad." Silent laughter vibrated from behind the row of white teeth as his smile widened at the angry red flags in her cheeks.

There was a feline desire for Cathie to sharpen her so-called claws across his cheekbone and add a few more scars to go with the small one near his right eye. A glance down at Tad's bewildered face halted the biting comment that sprang to her tongue.

"You misunderstood me, Mr. Douglas," she said forcing a smile to appear on her taut face. "I was only correcting you that I'm called Cathie and not Cat. If I sounded sharp I suppose that's the teacher in me."

"That's argumentative, but we won't discuss it now." There was still the sparkle of superior laughter in his eyes.

The infuriating presence of Rob Douglas succeeded in making her forget all others in her vicinity. Therefore Clay's greeting—"Hello, Tad, Cathie,"—caught her completely by surprise. There was a moment of expectancy as both men waited for Cathie to introduce them.

"This is Tad's father, Rob Douglas." She glanced at Clay, who had been studying her heightened color and was now turning his appraising gaze to Rob Douglas, the obvious cause of her anger. Clay smiled at the way the man's eyes were admiring Cathie's upturned profile. There were few men who wouldn't be moved by her unusual beauty. "This is my fiancé, Clay Carlsen," Cathie finished.

Her head tilted defiantly as she faced Rob Douglas again. There was an almost imperceptible raising of one dark brow.

"Carlsen?" his low voice questioned as he accepted the hand Clay offered.

"Cathie and I are distant cousins," Clay smiled.

"This is a very small and tight-knit community. You'll find that nearly all the families that have been here for a period of time are related to each other in one way or another." Cathie was angry with herself for making a further explanation. She and Clay shared the same last name, but there was certainly nothing incestuous about their relationship.

"I've heard that before," Rob nodded, a complacent smile remaining on his face as Cathie moved closer to Clay. "It must be very convenient. The only change you'll have to make is from Miss to Mrs., or are you the type that prefers Ms?" He didn't give either a chance to reply. "Whose grandparents was it that used to own my farm?"

Her teeth grated at his possessive pronoun.

"Cathie's," Clay answered for her.

"It's always belonged to a Carlsen ever since my great-grandfather bought it as unimproved prairie land over a hundred years ago." Angry pride forced her to stake her own claim on the farm that he called his.

A thoughtful look subdued the sparkle in his eyes as Rob studied her. "It must have been difficult to part with it after all these years. It's unfortunate that your grandfather didn't leave it to one of his children."

"My grandparents only had three children. Uncle Andrew was killed in a car accident when

I was a child." The feeling of injustice crept into her voice, although Cathie tried to explain the circumstances calmly. "My father is a professor at the university and my aunt's husband is a doctor. My grandfather didn't feel it was fair to saddle either of them with a farm, which is why he asked that it should be sold and the proceeds divided."

"Your grandfather must have been a practical man," Rob Douglas stated.

"The same can't be said for his granddaughter," Clay sighed, smiling as he put an arm around Cathie's shoulders. "She tried to persuade her father to buy the farm just to keep it in the family."

"I suppose the two of you could have lived on it once you were married to look after it for him." Rob voiced the same thought that Cathie had, but she found herself springing to Clay's defense rather than endorse his suggestion.

"Clay is an attorney. It wouldn't be fair to ask him to give up all those years of school to run the farm or to try to practice law at the same time as running the farm."

Rob Douglas intercepted Clay's look of surprise. Cathie held her breath in anticipation of some astute comment, but Rob made none.

"Tad and I have detained you two from your dinner long enough and I know Mrs. Carver is waiting for us," Rob stated, placing a hand on the shoulder of the boy standing patiently by his side. "It's been a pleasure meeting you, Miss Carlsen, and you, Clay."

Cathie didn't realize how rigidly she had been

holding herself until she and Clay were alone.
Then a trembling seized her legs as the after-
shock of meeting Rob Douglas set in.

CHAPTER FOUR

A MALE CARDINAL BUTTERFLY flitted across Cathie's path, his scarlet body and black-crowned head quickly disappearing amidst the branches of a flowering catalpa tree. Her white cotton sundress with its appliqués of daisies around the hem intensified the golden tan of her bared skin. She shifted the books she was carrying from one arm to the other. Beneath her leather sandals she could feel the burning heat of the pavement from the hot June sun. The asphalt in the streets was soft and mushy to the step. These were the days to enjoy the burning warmth of the sun before the scorching heat and high humidity of Iowa's July and August arrived.

Cathie was making her weekly trek to the local library, preferring to go in the middle of the week when there were fewer people and she had plenty of time to browse without interfering with anyone else. The last two books she read she hadn't enjoyed at all. Because of her meeting on Sunday with Rob Douglas, Cathie found herself picturing him as the leading male character in the novels, which had made it difficult to concentrate on the plots. She would have preferred to forget she had ever met him, but his image was too potent to wish away.

Her hand closed over the iron railing as Cathie started up the concrete steps that led into the small library. From the corner of her eye she glimpsed a group of children gathered at the end of the block. Their chanting voices pierced her semi-daydream state. Cathie halted midway up the steps as she recognized Tad Douglas in the center of the group. The jeering sound of the children's laughter angered Cathie and she retraced her way down the steps and started walking toward the white-faced boy so determinedly trying to ignore the taunts hurled at him.

But she wasn't the only one who had seen the harassment taking place. As Cathie walked closer to the group, she saw Rob Douglas walk out of the lumber store across the street, his bristling stride carrying him directly to the scene. He reached the group several steps before Cathie.

His growling demand, "What's going on here?" scattered the children in every direction, while Tad took one look at the scowl on his father's face and tucked his chin against his chest.

"What was all this about, Tad?" His stern words brought no response from the boy. Rob Douglas's hand shot out and twisted Tad's face up toward his. "I want an explanation."

Cathie knew that closed sullen look on his son's face. She had seen it often enough in class. Although she had the opportunity of turning away and avoiding another meeting with Rob Douglas, she chose not to take advantage of it.

Stepping forward, she said, "The other children were teasing him about his name."

The fiery dark eyes were turned on Cathie and she experienced relief that his anger wasn't directed at her. Rob looked all the more imposing in brown slacks and a tight-fitting knitted short-sleeved shirt. The muscular physique that his Sunday dress had only hinted at was revealed by his casual clothes.

"What do you mean, his name?" Rob Douglas released Tad's chin, which immediately fell back to his chest.

"Tad, short for tadpole or a frog." Cathie spoke quietly as if the softness of her voice would ease the pain those words had inflicted.

The grim line around Rob's mouth grew even grimmer as he looked down at the bent sandy-haired head of his son. He inhaled deeply to control his anger and glanced at Cathie. "I appreciate the information, Miss Carlsen. Good day."

After a brief nod in her direction, he herded Tad across the street to where his car was parked. Cathie watched them for a minute before turning back toward the library, trying to refocus her thoughts on choosing books, but finding Rob Douglas a potent influence on her mind.

"Aw, come on, Cathie," Andy wheedled. "You said yourself that Clay wasn't coming over tonight, so you have no reason for not coming with us to Black Hawk Lake."

"Really, Andy, I don't feel like going swimming tonight." Cathie refused for about the sixth time, and the second time since their evening meal. "I would rather spend a quiet night along here at the house."

"There's a whole group of us going. Nobody's matched.up with anyone else, so you don't need to worry about Clay getting jealous," the dark-haired girl persevered. "I agree that it's terribly peaceful with Connie on vacation at Okoboji, but it's too beautiful a night to sit around by yourself."

"That's exactly what I want to do," Cathie insisted.

"Well," said Andy, sighing as she lifted her shoulders in a resigned gesture, "if that's what you really want to do, far be it from me to try to change your mind. But you're really going to miss an awfully fun evening."

"I'll try to survive," Cathie replied drolly as she secured her blond hair behind her head with a tortoiseshell clasp.

A car horn tooted impatiently in front of the house. "That must be Mary Beth!" Andy exclaimed, racing out of the kitchen to the front room where her beach bag and towel were. As she retraced her steps, speeding toward the outside door, she called out to Cathie, "I don't know what time we'll be back, so don't worry if I'm late. Bye!" And the door slammed.

The oscillating fan continued to whir noisily from its position on the kitchen counter, so the house didn't become completely silent at the departure of Andy. Cathie stared at the closed door, her green eyes clouded and without their usual jewel-bright sparkle. Now that she was alone, she stopped fighting the restless feeling that had been nagging at her all afternoon and evening. The true reason she had declined Andy's invitation wasn't because she wanted to spend the evening alone, but because she didn't feel like going swimming with a boisterous and laughing group of people. Nor was she missing Clay's company, even though he was tied up this evening.

It was a strange mood she was in, unsettled, restless. There were plenty of things she could do—read one of the books she had picked up at the library today, write her parents a letter, do some washing. Cathie could think of all the things she could do, but nothing that she wanted to do.

After wandering aimlessly through the house twice and drawing concerned looks from the dog Duchess, Cathie finally picked up one of the library books and settled in an easy chair in the living room. It was a futile attempt because she kept reading the same page over and over without remembering what she had read. The ring of the telephone was almost a relief.

Lifting the black receiver, she said, "Hello."

"Hello. This is Rob Douglas. I wondered if you were free this evening?"

For a moment Cathie's heart stopped beating before it began racing away at an incredible speed. She collected herself before answering. "You must want Connie. She's on vacation. This is Cathie Carlsen speaking."

"I'm aware that Connie is on vacation and I know whom I'm speaking to." There was a suggestion of dry amusement in his voice. "It's you that I wish to see, Miss Carlsen."

"Me? What do you want to see me about?" A frown creased her forehead as her hand tightened its grip on the receiver.

"There are some personal things I want to discuss with you," Rob answered. "May I come over?"

"What personal things? About your son?" Cathie wanted it clarified before she would consider agreeing to another face-to-face confrontation with him. "Surely we can discuss it over the telephone?"

"I don't care to discuss my personal affairs over a party line. I'll be there in about twenty minutes."

"Just a moment, I—" she began, but the line on the other end was dead. Slowly she replaced the receiver on its hook, wishing that she had gone with Andy instead of staying home.

Then cold anger swept over her at his highhanded assumption that simply because he said he was coming over she would be there. He hadn't even waited for her to say whether she was free.

"Duchess, I think it's time someone taught Mr. Douglas a lesson." The dog's tail wagged briefly as if in agreement while Cathie hurried toward the small desk in the living room to retrieve some paper and a pencil. She quickly jotted down a note addressed to Rob Douglas that stated she had a previous engagement, then rummaged through the desk drawers to find some adhesive tape.

A wicked sparkle gleamed from her green eyes as she taped the message to the front door. She paused long enough to imagine Rob Douglas's face when he saw it before dashing back into the house for her handbag and the car keys inside it. After several minutes' delay trying to remember where she had left the bag, Cathie found it and sped out of the door to the small garage.

The heavy garage door was its usual stubborn self, opening halfway, then refusing to budge until Cathie had broken a sacrificial fingernail. Inside the car, she put the key in the ignition, listened to the motor turn over once, then twice, then three times before it finally coughed and sputtered into life. Excitement flushed her face, giving it a youthful vigor as she turned in the seat to look out of the back window and reverse the car out of the garage into the drive. Before she could maneuver the car into the street, a gold and brown El Dorado pulled into the driveway, effectively blocking her escape.

Her hand smote the steering wheel in anger. "Damn! Damn! Damn!" she muttered under her breath.

"Such language!" Rob Douglas' tongue clicked in mock scolding as he leaned down to look in the window on the driver's side. His mouth quirked at the furious expression on her face. It was not a smile, but pique touched by amusement at her futile attempt to elude him. "You surely didn't think it would take me twenty minutes to drive that distance? The farm is barely two miles from town."

"If you would read the note on the door, you'll find I have another engagement," she stated coldly. "So if you will kindly move your car, I'll be on my way."

He reached in the opened window, turned off the motor and extracted the key from the ignition, his arm brushing her rounded breast. "You're lying, Cat," he stated calmly. "You don't have any other appointment."

"And just how do you know that?" she demanded, refusing to reach for the keys that were being held just out of reach.

"If you legitimately had other plans for this evening, you would have seized on that excuse for not seeing me immediately. As it is, you only thought of it after I'd hung up," he smiled. The smile didn't lessen the hard, uncompromising glitter in his eyes. "I can't understand why you're so anxious to avoid me, Cat, especially since I only want to talk to you as parent to teacher."

"Stop calling me Cat!" She was bristling with anger as he opened the car door for her. Brushing away the hand he offered, Cathie stepped out of the car, seething with fury that he could see through her pretense so easily. "My keys, please."

Rob Douglas dropped them in her outstretched palm and Cathie transferred them to her bag. Her hands clenched the leather bag tightly as she stood silently in front of Rob, too aware of the way he towered over her. He looked so cool and collected in his creased plaid slacks and crisp gold shirt. She unnecessarily smoothed her hair back to where it was caught by the clasp, fighting to get control of her temper.

"I suppose we should go in the house," Cathie suggested icily.

"It would be more conducive to a business conversation than the hard cement of your front steps," he agreed, stepping aside so she could lead the way, a cool, arrogant gleam lighting his brown eyes as she stalked past him.

Duchess met Cathie at the door, her tail wagging until she saw the stranger following her mistress. A shrinking shyness sent the dog hiding behind Cathie's legs, the graying muzzle sticking out to test the air in case it was someone she knew.

"Your watchdog?" Dark eyebrows raised significantly.

Cathie wished it were true, then she could have set Duchess on him. Instead she sighed, "She's just a pet. She was my grandfather's dog, but she always was shy around strangers, and since I took her from the farm, the poor dear has been even worse." She gave the red gold head hugging her knees a reassuring pat. "Go and lie down, Duchess."

"She's a beautiful animal, even if she is beginning to show her age. An English shepherd, isn't she?"

"Yes," Cathie nodded abruptly. "Would you prefer the kitchen or the living room?"

"Wherever you think would be most comfortable."

There wasn't any room that would seem comfortable to Cathie as long as Rob Douglas was in it, but since he left it up to her, she chose the kitchen. Its strictly utilitarian atmosphere would not encourage casual conversation. With luck their discussion about Tad would be short and she could send him quickly on his way.

"Would you care for something to drink?" She didn't want to offer him anything, but her ingrained hospitality demanded it of her. "I could make some instant coffee, or I have pink lemonade in the refrigerator."

"Spare me the instant coffee," Rob refused firmly, revealing the same aversion she felt toward it. "But I will have some lemonade, if you don't mind."

"Not at all." Minutes later she set a glass for each of them on the formica-topped table and drew out a chair on the opposite side of the table from where he was seated. "Now, what did you want to discuss about Tad?" she requested in her most businesslike manner.

"You didn't seem surprised by the episode this afternoon. I take it this has happened before."

"Yes. It's not at all unusual for a child to be teased about his name. Another boy in my class is named Jack, but the children invariably call him Jack Rabbit because his ears stick out. It's something a teacher can't prevent." Cathie didn't have any intention of being blamed for it.

His thorough study of her face was making her uncomfortable. "I'm not accusing you of anything," Rob told her, looking unbearably relaxed and in charge. "How does he get along in school?"

"You signed his report card," she returned defensively. "He's an excellent student, as I said before."

"I don't doubt his scholastic ability," he agreed with marked patience. "I'm more concerned about his ability to get along with other children."

"Doesn't Tad talk about what goes on at school to you?" Cathie was unwilling to point out how singularly detached Tad had been from the rest of the class.

"I want your view."

"Very well," she took a deep breath. If he wanted her view, she would give it to him just exactly the way it was without any of the frills of teacher diplomacy. "Tad seemed to be determined not to become a part of the class. He never took part in any discussions, didn't join in any games unless he was forced to, and kept to himself at all other times. He was the straggler, the last one to arrive in the room and the last to leave. He avoided all contact that he could with the rest of the students." Cathie paused, taking in the grim set of Rob Douglas' jaw. He wasn't liking what he was hearing and there was a pleasing sense of revenge that she was upsetting him as much as he upset her. "Even the way he dressed, his expensive slacks, set Tad apart. They weren't the clothes for the rough and tumble play of boys."

"He didn't make any friends?" His gaze hardened and Cathie's eyes were drawn to the small scar, its pencil-thin line making the glitter in his dark eyes appear all the more portentous.

"None."

His hand closed tightly over the glass on the table. "Did you think his behavior was natural?"

"Of course not." An angry frown creased her forehead.

"Then why didn't you see fit to notify me of Tad's behavior?"

Cathie knew she had been wrong in that. If it had been anyone other than Rob Douglas, she would have contacted the parent. But she had been too determined not to have anything to do with him. Even now she couldn't admit that she was wrong.

"I believed that, given time, Tad would adjust," she answered primly. "After all, it wasn't just the school that was different. He had moved to a different state, had a new home, and I had heard that his mother died last fall. Those are quite a few changes for a small boy to adapt to, and I didn't think the two months of school was enough time for him to do it."

"But you still didn't think I needed to know what was going on." Rob shook his head in exasperation and anger. "Why?"

"I thought he would confide in you," Cathie flared. "You are his father!"

"Yes," he sighed, leaning against the padded chairback. Grim lines deepened the grooves around his mouth, determination etched in the carved lines. "I am his father."

"Surely you had some indication of what was going on?" The somber concern in his face made Cathie unconsciously soften her tone and take the sarcasm out of it.

Rob looked at her sharply from beneath the

dark gathering of his brow. "When you were listing the adjustments Tad has to make, you didn't include a father that he doesn't know."

"What?" Cathie breathed, her head tilted to the side in surprise, not quite sure she had heard him right.

"I met Tad's mother when she was only seventeen. She was a fey unworldly creature, unlike anyone I'd ever met. Her parents were extremely wealthy and owned a large estate on the east coast. When she told them she wanted to marry me, it was probably the only time in her life that she'd stood up to them. Since she wasn't of legal age, we needed their consent, and they would only give it if we agreed to live in the small guest house on the estate grounds." Rob continued in a flat, unemotional voice. "I won't embarrass you with the more intimate failures of our marriage except to say that when Yvette discovered she was pregnant, she used it as an excuse to move back to the main house. I stayed on. I thought when our child was born he would tie us together, but her parents, Yvette and Tad became the family and I was the one who was excluded."

In spite of herself Cathie felt a welling of sympathy for him, even though she realized he was too proud a man to accept it, if he ever needed it, which she doubted.

"We were divorced a year after Tad was born. The fey, unworldly charm that had attracted me to Yvette was the result of an excessively sheltered and controlled life. Her parents' world was conducted within the confines of the estate

walls, and because Yvette knew no other, she
saw no harm in raising our child in the same
way. At the time I had neither the money nor
the power her parents possess, so there was no
chance of taking my son away from her. I was
refused visiting privileges with Tad unless
Yvette or her parents were with me. The last
time I saw Tad he was five years old. He sat pas-
sively in a chair the whole time, dressed like a
miniature mannequin, not playing or showing
any desire to play. I didn't go back again until
Yvette's death last fall. It was worse than the
last time I saw him, and I knew it was my last
chance to get him away from that sterile, sup-
pressive environment. The court hearing took
place in February and the judge awarded me
custody. Only now is Tad beginning to doubt all
those stories he was told about how I didn't care
about him, that I'd deserted him and his mother.
So you see, that shell of hardened reserve he
protects himself with is a difficult thing to combat and this teasing by his classmates only
serves to reinforce it."

"Why are you telling me all this?" Her voice
was tight. She didn't want to know about his
past or that of his son. She didn't want to
become involved in his life, and yet some unseen
little voice kept telling her she already was, that
their paths were already entwined. "You should
be telling Mrs. Gleason, his new teacher."

Rob leaned forward to rest both arms on the
table and gaze intently at Cathie. "There are
three long months of summer vacation. Three
months during which you and I together could
help Tad take a giant step forward."

"Why me?" she protested, feeling herself being drawn into the whirlpool of his plans and wanting to resist, to shut her ears to his low, persuasive voice.

"Because Tad likes you. Your approval has become important to him. You haven't been sullied in his mind as I have by the name-calling of his grandparents. He can accept you as you are."

"I don't understand. What could I possibly do to help him?"

His gaze firmly held hers. "You told Tad once that you used to spend your summers on the farm. I can barely persuade him to walk in the barn door, and if it weren't for that little yellow kitten that lives in the barn, I wouldn't get him that far."

"And you think I might be able to talk him into being more adventurous," Cathie finished his thought.

"Let's put it this way. Tad is intrigued by the tree house in the grove opposite the house. He asked me once if I thought you used to play in it as a child, but he won't venture over there. Several other times he's inquired whether you might have done something or other when you were on the farm."

"So what are you asking? That I take him on a grand tour of the place?" She had to make her voice sarcastic to hide the ache in her heart brought on by her cherished memories of the Homeplace.

"To see it a few times through your eyes might make it seem less alien to Tad," Rob said quietly.

"That won't help him get along any better with the other children," Cathie pointed out desperately.

"If we can get Tad to accept his surroundings, we might be able to get him to accept the people that live here."

Why did he persist in coupling their names together, Cathie thought in irritation. "It's impossible," she said aloud, shoving her chair back from the table and rising to her feet.

"I'm not asking very much, only a few trips to the farm to visit my son." An eyebrow quirked arrogantly in her direction.

Put that way, it didn't sound like very much, and she would seem terribly churlish to refuse. "I'll do it," Cathie agreed ungraciously, "for Tad's sake."

"It never occurred to me that you would do it for any other reason," said Rob, an arrogant, mocking glitter in his eyes. He rose from his chair and walked over to the table near where Cathie was standing. She was looking out the window at the orange dusk laced with streaks of purpling pink, but she turned at his approach.

"Is that all you wanted, Mr. Douglas?" she demanded, glad of the shadows that prevented her from seeing his face clearly, all too aware of the thudding of her heart brought on by the resentment he always generated in her.

"Yes, that's all. I didn't think our discussion would take up so much time. I've really made you late for your so-called appointment now." Amusement lurked in his voice as Rob Douglas recalled her fictitious excuse when he had arrived.

"You know very well I had no such appointment," Cathie retorted sharply and bitterly, taking the now empty glass from his hand.

"You just didn't want my company, is that right?" That knowledge didn't seem to upset him too much.

"Yes, that is exactly right," she agreed, tilting her chin upward in defiance.

"I wonder why? Do you know?" He evidently meant his question to be rhetorical because he continued talking, a hand reaching out to hold Cathie's and examine the diamond ring on her third finger. "You don't have the look of a woman in love," he mused. "When is the wedding?"

"We haven't set a date yet, if it's any of your business."

"What day would you like to come out to the farm?" Rob asked, ignoring the deliberate snub.

He was pinning her down, as if he doubted that she would keep her word to come out. "Would next Tuesday be convenient?" she inquired haughtily, knowing she was delaying the time for as long as she could to give herself an opportunity to gather her defenses around her before she had to meet up with him again.

"Around one-thirty would be fine," Rob agreed, taking his leave of her.

CHAPTER FIVE

THE WILD ROSES were in bloom along the roadside, their pink petals accented by the green, green grasses. A wild canary flew among the grove of trees, his yellow body like a shaft of sunlight in the shade. The familiar cry of a meadowlark sounded in the distance. There was that indescribable feeling of coming home as Cathie turned her car into the farm lane. Even Duchess recognized it, becoming a whining, wiggling mass of ecstasy from her place in the back seat.

The dog tumbled out of the car the minute Cathie parked it and opened the door. Her russet gold and white body was a quivering mass of happiness as she raced from the car to the house and back again. Her feathery tail that had seemed to be perpetually tucked between her legs since Cathie had taken Duchess away from the farm was now wagging merrily in the air. A tightness gripped Cathie's throat because she knew her heart gave a similar leap of joy when she gazed around the familiar and beloved surroundings.

This was her second visit with Tad. The first she had kept short so she could ease out of the role of teacher. Rob Douglas had not mentioned that Cathie was going to visit them, and Tad had been pleased and surprised when she did. Much of his reserve vanished at the discovery that she had stopped to see him and not anyone else. They had taken a short walk around the house and yard with an excursion across the road to the grove of trees where the tree house was, but Cathie wasn't able to persuade Tad to climb the tree for a closer look. She was glad that his father had been out in the fields and she hadn't had to encounter him during the visit. It had made it all the more enjoyable for her.

It looked as if she wasn't going to be as lucky on this visit as Rob Douglas followed his son out of the house. Duchess intercepted them as they reached the halfway point between the house and Cathie. The dog sniffed Tad's feet before greeting the boy enthusiastically, much to Cathie's delight. She had always known the shepherd liked children, but she had particularly been anxious that the dog make friends with Tad. The boy was hesitant to touch the red gold head until a quiet word from his father prompted the movement. Duchess attached herself proprietorially to Tad's heels and accompanied him to Cathie.

"Good afternoon, Miss Carlsen. Tad told me you came last week," Rob Douglas greeted her smoothly without even a gleam of conspiracy in his eyes.

"How do you do, Mr. Douglas," she returned before turning to smile at Tad. "Hi, Tad. I see you've met Duchess. I hope you don't mind my bringing her along, but she was terribly homesick for the farm. She used to live here, too."

"She seems to be a very nice dog," Tad observed solemnly, gazing down at the graying muzzle that was turned adoringly toward him.

"If you two will excuse me," Rob broke in, "I have a lot of work to be done and I'm sure you want to plan what you're going to do this afternoon."

Cathie breathed a silent sigh of relief as he walked away. She was always so stiff and uncomfortable around him, as if she were constantly holding her breath in anticipation of something. Besides, he was so infuriatingly male.

"As you can see by the way I'm dressed," Cathie began brightly the minute Rob was out of hearing, "I thought I'd take you on a tour of some of the places where I used to play."

Tad inspected her patched blue jeans and the scuffed tennis shoes, passing over the faded red-checked blouse to stop on her face.

"Do you have some old clothes to change into?" she asked. She could tell from the doubtful expression on his face that the neat slacks and bright print shirt were repeated in the rest of his wardrobe. She could have bitten off her tongue for making such a mistake. "It doesn't matter," Cathie hurried on. "I don't imagine we'll get all that messed up just walking."

"Maybe we can go fishing instead," Tad suggested with marked hesitation. "You told me the last time that you used to do that lots of times and I've never been fishing. Do you suppose we could, Miss Carlsen?"

"School is out, Tad. You can call me Cathie."

The smile on her face was genuine, but it didn't reassure the boy.

"I was always told that it wasn't proper to call your elders by their first name," he said solemnly, his eyes gazing earnestly into the depths of her green ones.

"That's old-fashioned. Besides, you make me feel like an old maid," Cathie teased, drawing the smile from his face that she had been seeking. "And I think fishing is a great idea. I'm sure my old poles are still in the garage. I'll go and check while you run in and ask Mrs. Carver if she has a container of some sort that we can put worms in."

Tad was off like a flash with Duchess running excitedly beside him, while Cathie walked to the large double garage. There, amid the open rafters, she spied the old bamboo poles that she and Clay had used so many times before. It took a few tricky maneuvers before she was able to get them down. Surprisingly the hooks weren't rusted and the red and white bobbers, although a little dirty, were still serviceable. There was a garden spade leaning against the corner of the garage and Cathie picked it up and joined Tad in the front yard. He was trying to appear as calm and self-possessed as always, but Cathie saw the glimmer of excitement in his hazel eyes.

"The next stop is for Mr. Worm," she announced gaily as Tad proudly held an empty coffee can out for her to see.

"Where do we find him?"

"In the ground, silly," she laughed. "Out behind the machine shed is the best place."

"Which one is the machine shed?" Ted asked, glancing around at the mixture of buildings that comprised the barnyard.

"That one there by the drive where your dad keeps his tractors and plows," Cathie pointed. They set off toward it with Duchess trotting contentedly alongside.

"What's that big white building next to it?"

Cathie smiled to herself. At last he was expressing an interest in his new home, and she felt slightly guilty for being the person he asked instead of his father. "That's the corn crib. Do you see the weather vane on top of the cupola?" Tad nodded. "The direction the rooster is facing tells us which way the wind is blowing. Today it's from the west. 'When the wind is from the west, the fish bite the best,' " she chanted, remembering the old rhyme that had been her and Clay's byword.

"Do you really think we'll catch some fish?"

"The Boyer has a lot of catfish, bullheads and carp in it. And if we can find us some worms, I don't know why we won't."

"What's the Boyer?"

"That's the name of the river that runs through the pasture," Cathie explained patiently as they rounded the corner of the machine shed. Propping the fishing poles against the side of the building, she carried the spade over to where some old lumber was piled. "Help me lift this plank, Tad."

Once the board was lifted and set on top of some others, she set about digging up clumps of moist, black sod. She smiled to herself as Tad rather hesitantly helped her break up the clumps and capture the quicksilver worms trying to escape.

"I think that's enough," she said, glancing into the coffee can where fat, wriggling worms tried to bury themselves in the few chunks of earth she had thrown in.

"My hands are all dirty." He was staring at them and the slime and dirt that coated them. "I'd better go and wash."

Cathie checked herself just in time from saying that his hands were going to get a lot dirtier. "If you rub your hands together like this," she showed him, "you can get the worst of it off and we can rinse the rest off in the water trough."

Reluctantly Tad followed her suggestion while Cathie knocked the dirt off the spade and set it to the front of the machine shed so she could carry it back to the garage when they returned. It was difficult not to watch his meticulous efforts to clean as much of the grime off as possible. It was a strain on the imagination that here was a boy who didn't like to get dirty, but Cathie kept her amusement concealed.

"Are you ready?" she called, picking up the bamboo poles and resting them against her shoulder.

With a skeptical look in his eye, Tad picked up the can of worms and joined Cathie. Together they set off toward the pasture gate, pausing at the concrete water trough to rinse off their hands. Instead of taking the gate that led into the pasture, Cathie chose to walk the rutted track along the pasture fence line that bordered the cornfield.

"Why aren't we going that way?" Tad inquired, hopping to keep up with her longer strides.

"I was getting thirsty, and if we go this way, we can stop off at the spring for a drink." Cathie was determined to introduce Tad to all the simple treasures of the farm. "Here's the spring." She stopped, pointing to the sliver of gleaming silver water on the other side of the fence. "You go first, Tad."

Stepping on the bottom strand of barbed wire with her tennis shoe, Cathie held the top strand up for Tad to crawl through. She was a bit more of an expert at dodging the thorny wire and wiggled through on her own.

Clumps of grass were sneaking onto the pebble strewn area surrounding the tile through which the spring water came, but there was still enough open dry sand for Cathie to kneel on and scoop up handfuls of the refreshing water. She stepped back and watched Tad mimic her movements.

"Mmm, that's really cold," he declared, wiping the driplets of water from his mouth with the back of his hand. "Almost colder than the water Mrs. Carver keeps in the refrigerator."

Tad's grimy hands were forgotten as he once again entered into the spirit of adventure. The dullness was gone from his hazel eyes, making them sparkle with gold flecks introduced by the brilliance of the sun. He picked up the can of worms and set out with Cathie to follow the tiny ribbon of spring water to where it joined the Boyer River. There was an unaccustomed lightness in his walk that brought a satisfied smile to her face.

At any place they could have stepped across the rivulet of water, but Cathie led him to the weeping willow tree whose main trunk lay horizontally over the spring. "Follow me," she ordered, glancing back at the boy behind her as she began her balancing walk across the rough bark of the trunk. A foot or so on the other side of the spring, the trunk began rising upward to the sun, and that was where Cathie hopped off onto the ground.

Tad followed a bit more slowly, but landed on the ground near her with a proud smile of accomplishment on his face. Where the spring dumped into the river, the water was smooth, reflecting the bright sun like a mirror. A multitude of wild flowers dotted the pasture grass with honey bees busily gathering their sweet nectar. Cathie felt incredibly like a child again as she led Tad along the river bank on one of the many trails the cattle had carved into the hillside.

"The cows won't bother us, will they?" Tad inquired, glancing across the river where a scattered group of dairy cows was grazing.

"No, they're gentle," Cathie assured him in an offhand manner to lend emphasis to her words. They were approaching the singing rapids. "We'll cross the river here, that way we can fish on the other side where the water is deeper and have the sun at our backs."

"How are we going to get across?"

The poles were already lying on the ground as

Cathie bent to remove her tennis shoes. "We'll wade. The water is only a foot or so deep. Clay used to be able to cross with his shoes on by hopping from stone to stone. Every time I tried, my foot slipped into the water and I got my shoes wet. Now I play it safe by taking them off."

As soon as her shoes and socks were off and her jeans rolled up, Cathie turned to help Tad, showing him how to tie the laces of his shoes together so he could carry them around his neck. Then the pair waded into the bubbling water racing over the collection of rocks. After his first hesitant steps and exclamations of the water's coolness, Tad enjoyed the refreshing and uninhibited sensation of the swiftly running river curling around his ankles. They paused at the small sandbar sitting in the middle of the river, a partial cause of the rapids, and Cathie pointed out a school of minnows gathered in the protective shallow waters.

The teacher instinct was strong and unwittingly she began turning the excursion into a biology trip, starting with the minnows, then the snails and explaining the functions of other larger fish in the balance of nature in the river. His inquisitive mind readily took to the subject, his questions continuing as they stopped on the opposite bank to wipe their wet feet with their socks and put their shoes back on.

"Where does this river go?"

"It flows on south and dumps into the Missouri River north of Omaha, Nebraska. Did you know, Tad, that the state of Iowa has the mighty

Mississippi River as its eastern boundary and most of the muddy Missouri River at its western boundary? And the waters from this very river end up in the Gulf of Mexico."

Arriving at the spot where she had decided they would fish, Cathie slid down the steep bank to a lower shelf, then took the can of worms from Tad and helped him down. The geography lesson was set aside as Cathie showed him the fine art of putting a protesting worm on a hook. Her distaste of the job was similar to his but, as she explained, necessary if they wanted to catch any fish. An expert cast was easy with the bamboo poles and soon they were both leaning against the black soil of the bank watching the red and white bobbers floating on the dark waters of the river.

"Once Clay and I decided to make a raft and float all the way down to the mouth of the Mississippi River. We launched it up on the river by that far island." She was resting her chin on her knees as she indicated an island upriver.

"How far did you get? Did you go all the way?" Tad asked eagerly, caught up by the excitement of the idea.

"Clay and I weren't very good boat-builders," Cathie laughed. "Tree houses and huts were more our line. The raft sank the very minute it went into the water."

"You must have really had a lot of fun here," Tad sighed, resting his chin on his knees in mimicry of Cathie.

She wanted to convince him that he could have a lot of fun, too, but that was something he had to realize himself. "What was it like where you used to live?" she asked, changing the subject to get Tad's comparison to his previous home and the farm.

"It was different. A lot different." A scowl covered his young face as he concentrated his gaze on the hypnotically bobbing bobber. "There were flowers and roses all over the lawns and gigantic trees and hedges all over. It was beautiful, like a painting. I picked some flowers once for my mother, but they were prize flowers or something. Everybody was really mad at me. I don't suppose I could have ever had a tree house there. My grandfather told me the oak trees were hundreds of years old and very valuable. Most all the furniture in the house was antique, even the bed I slept in. Grandmother was always afraid I would scratch it, but I never did. My mother's room was the most beautiful of all. Some nights she used to let me come in and sit while she listened to records."

"Do you like music?" Hearing Tad's calm acceptance of such a stifling existence, Cathie had to seize on an unrelated subject.

Tad nodded vigorously. "My favorite record that mother sometimes played was the '1812 Overture'. I liked it when the cannons boomed."

At his age, Cathie thought to herself, she probably would have been humming "Found a Peanut" instead of that, but at least he had exhibited a typically boyish reaction in his reasons for liking the song.

The bobber on Tad's line disappeared underwater for a split second before reappearing. "I think you have a nibble," Cathie whispered. "Watch your bobber."

It disappeared again and popped back to the surface. Tad gripped the pole tightly in his hands, glancing excitedly at Cathie, but unsure of what to do.

"Let the bobber go under again and give the pole a hard yank when it does," she instructed.

The bobber went under again and stayed. Cathie knew the fish was hooked and Tad wouldn't have to worry about setting the hook. They were both shouting with glee when Tad flipped the line out of the water and sent a good-sized bullhead flopping onto the grass of the upper bank. Removing hooks from fishes' mouths had never been Cathie's forte, but she managed to show Tad how it was done. While he rebaited his hook, she found a stick that would work as a stringer for their catch.

Now that the first fish had been caught, Tad set about his fishing in earnest. Their luck was evenly dispersed, with Tad catching two more and Cathie hooking three, one of which she tossed back as being too small. Both of them were enjoying themselves so much that the sound of a pickup truck blended in with the calls of the meadowlarks and crows, the distant babbling of the water over the rapids and the occasional lowing of the cows.

Both were surprised when Rob's voice sounded above them. "I saw you two from the road. Are you catching anything?"

Tad was the first to recover, jumping to his feet and scrambling up the steep bank without any concern for the condition of his clothes.

"I caught three bullheads!" he cried, unable to conceal his delight. "And Cathie caught three, too, but she put one back because it was too small to eat. Show him what we caught."

Quite willingly Cathie turned away from those brilliant brown eyes belonging to Rob Douglas to retrieve the makeshift stringer from the shallow water near the bank. She held them up for Rob to view, conscious of her racing pulse and the slight flush in her cheeks.

"Cathie said Mrs. Carver might cook them for supper tonight. Do you think she would?" Tad asked after Rob had suitably complimented his son on the size of the fish.

"I think we can persuade her," he nodded, turning an impersonal smile of gratitude on Cathie at this change in his son. "Don't you, Miss Carlsen?"

"I think so," Cathie agreed, only to be interrupted by Tad.

"She said to call her Cathie because Miss Carlsen makes her sound like an old maid," he announced, correcting his father, while Cathie made a mental wish to have a bit of his reticence for conversation retained, especially in the light of the laughing look in Rob's eyes.

"I think it's only fair that you call me Rob," he grinned. Cathie nodded agreement with a resigned smile, experiencing a flash of temper for ever agreeing to his proposition to show Tad around the farm. Immediate chagrin replaced her anger at the happy look on Tad's face. So far the experiment had been successful. "By the way," Rob went on, "I brought a bottle of lemonade and some cookies down with me just on the off chance that you two might be hungry or thirsty."

Since no one would suffer by her refusal but herself, Cathie accepted the offer of refreshments, knowing the effects of the sun and the soaring temperature had reduced her mouth to a cottony state.

"I didn't think to bring any glasses," Rob remarked, uncapping the quart bottle of lemonade and passing it to Cathie. "So it will have to be a community jar."

The sweetly tart liquid was truly thirst quenching as its tangy coldness soothed her parched throat. "Mmm, that's delicious," Cathie sighed, handing it back to Rob.

"Where were you going, father?" Tad asked, after he had taken a giant swig of the lemonade.

"Out to check on the new calves," Rob replied. "You haven't seen them yet, Tad. Would you like to come along?"

His son didn't reply, but turned instead to Cathie. "Did you used to do that?"

"Clay and I could hardly wait until the calves were born." All the other times she had referred to Clay that day, it had been a simple coupling because of the many childhood episodes they had enjoyed together, but this time Cathie knew his name was a defense mechanism to prevent Rob from drawing her more tightly into his family circle. "My grandpa always let us name them."

"Then you would be interested in this year's spring crop." Rob's dark gaze held hers as she swallowed nervously. "Since Clay isn't here—" there was a mocking twitch at the corner of his mouth "—you and Tad can name them."

"What about the fish?" his son interrupted, much to Cathie's relief.

"We can pick them up on the way back." Rob smiled down at the boy. "The five you caught are a pretty good size, just right for tonight's supper. So there's no need to catch any more. They'll wait there until the next time you go fishing."

His father's explanation assured Tad and he said, "All right, we'll go."

Cathie pressed her lips tightly together as the tall brown head turned toward her. She was being cornered into going with them and she didn't like it one bit.

"I'll have to pass," she said, smiling falsely into the velvet-brown eyes that were regarding her with amusement. "It's getting late and I really should go."

"It won't take more than a few minutes to check the calves." Rob's voice was soft and ultimately persuasive, but it only made Cathie harden her resolve. "And it will save you a walk all the way back to the house."

Her mouth opened to emit a polite refusal when she spied the stricken look on Tad's face. His shoulders were beginning to sag. Instead of their afternoon ending on a high point, her refusal was bringing back the boy's brittle shell.

"I'll go," Cathie gave in, tossing her head like an unruly filly as she glanced angrily at the smooth bronzed features looking so smugly back at her.

"Let's go, then." Rob smiled at his son, sending Cathie a sideways mocking glance. "Everybody in the truck."

"May I sit by the window?" Tad's exuberance had returned as he hopped around to the passenger's side of the cab.

Cathie inhaled deeply before agreeing, knowing that would place her in the middle beside Rob. But it was a typical request and she had no cause to deny Tad the window seat. If only she hadn't become so fond of the boy, she thought to herself, none of this would be happening.

The close quarters of the truck were stifling. It was impossible with the three of them in the seat for Cathie to avoid coming in contact with the driver. The brushing of his arm and thigh against hers transmitted a throbbing heat to her. Her pulse had quickened as Cathie held herself rigidly in the seat. The vague, resilient aroma of after-shave lotion mingled with his earthy, masculine scent to form an intoxicating combination. She stared straight ahead, trying to keep from bouncing into Rob as the truck made its slow, bumpy way over the uneven pasture ground.

The Boyer River snaked through the el-shaped pasture, its waters dividing it into two halves. A small herd of stock cows were occupying the far end of the el, and Cathie blinked in relief as the ivory-white hides of the Charlois-Angus herd came into view. Rob stopped the truck some distance away so as not to upset the quietly grazing cows and the trio climbed out of the cab. Cathie stayed near Tad while Rob walked closer, studying the cows and the calves. Several minutes later he walked back to them, his face a study in concentration.

"I have a calf missing," he announced. Now his eyes were diamond bright as they swept over the herd.

"Are you sure?" Cathie asked, knowing it was not uncommon for rustling to occur even in this day and age, although usually in numbers of more than one.

"Yes, I'm sure," Rob nodded. "The cow's probably hidden it somewhere."

"What are you going to do?" Tad inquired, his curiosity aroused by this interesting development.

"Find it, I hope, son," he replied, clasping the boy's shoulder warmly. "Want to give me a hand?"

"Sure," Tad nodded eagerly.

Rob turned to Cathie. "It will only take a few minutes. Will you help?"

"Yes," she answered. She was too much of a farm girl to refuse, especially for something as undemanding as finding a calf.

"We can be fairly sure the cow didn't hide the calf near the river because the cover isn't very good there. And she didn't hide it in this general area or she would have showed some interest when we drove up. That leaves the stretch of ground by the fence," Rob declared. "We'll fan out. If she starts following one of us then we'll find out where she's hidden the calf." He glanced down at Cathie. "I'll take Tad with me."

"Okay," she said, finding herself in complete agreement with his suggestion which, by its very thoroughness, let her know that he wasn't an inexperienced city-dweller.

The trio walked together for several yards until they reached the designated stretch of pasture. Then they split up with Tad and Rob veering to the left while Cathie changed her angle slightly toward the right.

"The cow has noticed us," Rob called. Cathie glanced over her shoulder to see the beige white cow alertly watching them. "She's concentrating on you, Cathie. The calf must be in your direction."

Maintaining the direction of her steps, she kept a close watch on the cow, anxious to find the exact location of the calf but cautious of incurring the wrath of the mother. Another glance over her shoulder saw the cow following her at a slow but interested pace. Cathie kept studying the terrain in front of her, trying to catch some sign of the calf without any success. A sound behind her drew another glance. The cow was trotting now, still several hundred feet away but coming closer. Quickening her pace, Cathie adjusted the direction she was walking so she would reach the fence in a shorter time.

But the change of direction was a mistake that she learned only after she had committed herself. The pace of the hoofbeats behind her increased and Cathie broke into a run, heading for a gap in the fence where the wires sagged. She kept telling herself not to panic, that there was no danger of the cow catching her as she ducked beneath the wires into the tall weeds on the other side of the fence.

Instantly the ground exploded beneath her. The air was rent by Cathie's shriek of surprise and the frantic bellowing of the calf she had just stepped on. As she dove headlong into the bull nettle, the calf made a hasty exit back into the pasture and his mother. The low, rolling sound of Rob's laughter intermixed with the more shrill sound of Tad's. Trying to avoid the prickles of the nettle bush, Cathie rolled into a cocklebur plant. When she finally regained her feet with the prickly burrs encased in her blouse and hair and the sting of the itchweed on her bare skin, she was livid with rage at the laughing pair walking toward her.

CHAPTER SIX

"ARE YOU ALL RIGHT?" Rob asked, trying to hide the chuckle in his voice with concern, but the laughter danced out of his eyes.

"A cow chases me through a fence and I land on the calf, fall into some itchweed and then a cocklebur patch and you ask if I'm all right!" Cathie snapped angrily.

"You were so funny," Tad giggled behind his hand.

She glanced from one to the other before looking down at her grass- and dirt-stained pants and blouse. Her sense of humor was too strong now that the shock of the situation was over.

"It must have looked pretty ridiculous," she conceded with a slight smile.

"I don't know who was more surprised, you or the calf." Rob grinned as Cathie broke into laughter. Tad immediately joined her, no longer holding back the giggles that were shaking his slender body.

As she imagined the comedy episode viewed from their eyes, tears of laughter blurred her vision as she tried to scramble back through the fence. Without the threat of the cow breathing down her neck, she got hung up on the barbs and Rob had to help her.

"Here, let me pick some of those burrs off you," Rob offered once she stood safely on the other side.

The laughter had at last subsided, leaving her short of breath. "I must look a sight." Cathie put a hand to her disheveled hair and encountered a prickly burr.

"I think you look beautiful," Rob said huskily from his position near her right shoulder.

She turned her brilliant jewel-green eyes up to his face, meeting the enigmatic expression in the fire of his dark eyes. No one had ever looked at her like that before—probing, somehow sensuous. Her heart hammered against her rib cage as she watched the hypnotic darkening of the brown eyes. This was just a reaction from the cow chasing her, Cathie told herself, although she didn't really believe a word of it. An ever-reddening flush filled her cheeks as she turned abruptly away from him.

"You sure found that calf in a hurry," Tad commented, his previously reserved face transformed by a grin that spread from ear to ear.

"I sure did," Cathie agreed, discovering it was hard to squeeze the words out through the lump in her throat.

"I think we could use some more of that lemonade, Tad. Why don't you run back to the truck and get it?" Before Cathie could suggest that they all go back, Rob directed his next order to her. "Stand still. I almost have all the cockleburs off your blouse."

Tad was speeding away and she was left alone with Rob. "Have you got them yet?" she asked, wishing he wouldn't stand so close to her. His nearness seemed to be having the oddest effect on her breathing.

"There are a few in your hair. I'd better get them out before they snarl these spun-gold locks of yours." There was a teasing quality to his voice that added to the small tremors running through her body. His touch was electric as he carefully worked the spiny burrs free from her hair. She could feel the caressing quality of his breath against her neck, a decidedly pleasing sensation that Cathie closed her eyes tightly against. "You have very beautiful hair, Cat," Rob murmured from somewhere near her ear. "Long hair has always seemed so totally feminine to me."

Some magic spell had wrapped its charms around her so she couldn't even take offense at his diminutive "Cat." As she felt herself about to capitulate completely to him, Cathie took a firm hold on herself. She was behaving like Andy would.

"Have you got them all out yet?" she asked in a voice that wasn't as shaky as she felt.

There was a hesitation before he answered. "Yes, that's the last, unfortunately."

"Here comes Tad with the lemonade." From her side vision, she had seen the boy approaching. Cathie willingly used him as an excuse to step away from Rob, nervously brushing the hair away from her face. "I can definitely use a cold drink after this."

After each had taken a drink from the jar, the trio started back to the pickup, with Cathie walking with Tad a step or two ahead of Rob. She was more grateful than she could say when Tad offered her his seat by the window and he took her place in the middle. She was much more at ease with the breeze from the opened window playing over her face as opposed to the burning touch of Rob Douglas. He stopped at their fishing hole and tossed the poles and bait in the rear of the truck while Tad took possession of their catch.

Duchess had long ago returned to the yard and barked a welcome at their arrival. Cathie was all set to climb in her car and leave, but Rob had noticed her idle scratching of her bare arms and insisted that she come into the house and wash in a solution of baking soda and water to take some of the sting away from the nettles.

"There's no need. I'll take care of it when I get home," she protested, sidling toward her car door.

His hand reached out and imprisoned her upper arm. "I insist," he said with a half-smile.

Her muscles stiffened and his grip tightened in response. It was a test of wills that Cathie would have fought to the finish if Tad hadn't been looking on. The glimmer of battle was in her eyes for Rob to see as she agreed.

Mrs. Carver was standing at the head of the steps as they entered the house. "There's a telephone call for you," she told Rob. "It's that man from the lumberyard about that material you ordered."

"Cathie fell in some nettles. I brought her in so she could wash off with some baking soda,"

Rob explained as he excused himself to answer the phone.

"Those nettles can really make you itch." The housekeeper clucked her tongue in sympathy, although Cathie had only noticed a mild reaction, probably because her mind had been so occupied with Rob Douglas and escaping his attention. "You wait here on the sun porch."

It was something of a relief to find the sun porch hadn't changed very much. The furniture was different, with a plumply cushioned, blue-flowered chaise longue near the windows and an assortment of similarly cushioned wicker furniture painted white. But the room ostensibly maintained the same airy atmosphere as when her grandparents had lived in the house. There was even a cribbage board on one of the small tables.

The door leading into the living room was closed, so she had no way of knowing what changes had been made there, if any. Naturally the kitchen remained the same. Of course it had already been modernized several years ago, which only left the repainting of walls or new curtains.

Mrs. Carver was back in a matter of minutes, carrying a washbowl, cloth and towel. The solution eased the mild stinging itch as Rob said it would. By the time Cathie had dried her arms with the towel, Rob still hadn't returned, so she asked Mrs. Carver to pass on her goodbyes and scurried out of the house.

Tad was in the yard playing with Duchess, tossing sticks that she was obligingly returning.

"Are you leaving?" Taking the stick from the shepherd and holding it in his hand, Tad studied her sadly.

"It's time I went home," Cathie nodded, adding with a smile, "but I'll come back another time."

"Would you like to stay for supper and have some of the fish we caught? I'm sure Mrs. Carver wouldn't mind." There was so much adult politeness in his invitation that Cathie almost wished she could stay to keep bringing out the little boy in him.

"No, not this time," she shook her head firmly. "Come on, Duchess," she called to the dog. "It's time for us to leave."

The shepherd trotted obediently to her side, but as they walked toward the car, Duchess lagged farther and farther behind. When Cathie opened the back door for the dog to climb in, Duchess stopped completely, her tail tucked between her legs and her pointed nose almost touching the ground.

"I don't think she wants to leave," Tad spoke.

At the sound of the boy's voice, Duchess slunk toward him, casting furtive glances behind her when Cathie ordered her back. The back screen door slammed. Cathie, who had been walking toward the dog hiding behind Tad's legs, glanced up to see Rob striding toward them. Duchess also saw the two adults converging on her and decided that the small boy didn't offer much protection. With a spurt of rebellion, the dog ignored the commands from Cathie and raced for the comparative safety of the little-used front porch and squeezed through a hole in the foundation.

"She won't come out from there until dark," Cathie sighed in exasperation.

"I guess she still considers this her home." Rob glanced down at her troubled expression, his innate awareness sensing her nervous desire to leave quickly.

"I'm afraid so."

"Does that mean we can keep her?" Tad piped up from behind them.

"Duchess belongs to Cathie, Tad," Rob corrected his son gently.

In her heart, Cathie disagreed, knowing that the dog belonged to the Homeplace, the farm. "Perhaps in the morning you'll be able to catch her," she said aloud.

"I'll bring her to you when I do," Rob assured her.

"Thank you. I'm sorry to put you to this trouble, but I never dreamed this would happen when I brought Duchess out here. A lot of things she's been, but never disobedient."

"It's no trouble." Cathie wasn't capable of meeting his gaze. Her nerves were too raw from their encounter in the pasture. The noncommittal look in his eyes told her he knew it as he held her car door open. "It will be a pleasure," he added.

Any softening in her attitude because she felt she was inconveniencing him was immediately erased by the infuriating realization that he could somehow read her mind. An eyebrow arched haughtily above a jade-green eye.

"You seem to forget, Mr. Douglas, that I'm engaged," Cathie reminded him none too gently, while making sure the ring on her left hand reflected the rays of the afternoon sun.

"No, I haven't forgotten, Miss Carlsen." Rob's mouth moved in a semblance of a smile as he shut the door and stepped back. "Have you?"

His reflection remained in her rearview mirror until Cathie made the turn out of the driveway onto the country road. He was absolutely insufferable, she told herself, so sure of his attraction that he thought every woman would fall at his feet. His casual flirting with her when he knew she was engaged added more fuel for her fiery temper.

There was only time for a hasty shower before Andy and Connie arrived at the house from work. The kitchen was stifling hot and Cathie knew it would be unbearable if she cooked anything on the stove. There was a fresh head of lettuce in the refrigerator, some leftover ham and chicken, a small bowl of hard-boiled eggs and two tomatoes. Add to that some cubes of cheddar cheese and she would have an adequate salad for their meal.

Later, after her roommates had returned home and the meal had been eaten, it was Connie who first commented on Duchess's absence.

"I see you've finally got rid of that mongrel," she observed, stepping into the hallway where the dog usually laid while Andy began the task of clearing away the dishes. "I was constantly finding dog hairs on my clothes, not to mention the odor that clung to everything."

"I haven't got rid of Duchess," Cathie corrected her sharply.

"You should," Connie sniffed, walking briskly from the room.

"Where is she?" Andy asked. "Is she sick?"

"No, nothing like that." Cathie hesitated, finding herself unwilling even to confide to Andy exactly where Duchess was. But lies had always caught up with her in the past. "I went out to the Homeplace today to see Tad. I took Duchess along and she hid from me when it was time to come home."

"Oh, no! So what are you going to do? You can't leave her out there."

"Tad's father is going to bring her back tomorrow."

"The poor dear probably thought she was going home for good," Andy commented, turning on the taps and filling the sink with soapy water. "What time is Mr. Douglas coming?" There was a merry twinkle in her dark eyes. "Now that he's evidently dropped Connie I might take a whirl at landing him myself!"

"I imagine he'll bring her back in the morning," Cathie answered, anxious to get off the subject of Rob Douglas.

"Naturally he'll come when I'm at work," Andy moaned.

Rob Douglas didn't bring Duchess back in the morning or the afternoon. Cathie had decided that they hadn't been able to catch the dog and was toying with the idea of calling to find out when Clay arrived to take her out to the theater.

"Are you ready to go?" he queried, dropping her an affectionate peck on her tanned cheeks.

"In a minute," she smiled, walking toward the telephone. "I was just going to call out to the farm to see if they've caught Duchess yet."

"The farm? Do you mean the Homeplace?" His forehead became creased with a curious frown. "What is Duchess doing out there?"

"I took her out there yesterday for a run when I called to see Tad," she answered calmly as she picked up the receiver.

Cathie knew Clay was averse to her decision to visit the boy now that school was out. Feeling that Rob had told her of his past marriage in confidence, she hadn't mentioned the true circumstances to Clay. He felt it was no longer her concern how the boy adjusted since he wouldn't be in her class in the autumn.

"He's here!" Andy squeaked, bounding into the living room via the kitchen hall. "He just drove up this minute!"

"Who?" Clay asked, but Cathie already knew.

"Rob Douglas," Andy informed Clay.

Cathie had already replaced the receiver and had turned toward the door. "Does he have the Duchess with him?" she asked, wiping the nervous sweat that had suddenly collected in the palm of her hands on the sides of her pink linen dress.

"Yes, I caught a glimpse of her in the back seat of his car," Andy told her, tagging along behind Clay and Cathie.

Rob was just getting out of his car when the three walked out the front door. A hand raised in greeting to them before coaxing the reluctant shepherd out of the car.

"Duchess doesn't seem very happy to be back," Clay commented when Cathie took the leash from Rob and nearly pulled the dog toward her.

"If you think she's unhappy, you should see Tad," Rob smiled, taking the hand that Clay offered in greeting. "He was practically heartbroken when I put the dog in the car."

If that was supposed to make Cathie feel guilty, it succeeded, combined with the very slight wag of the dog's tail when she petted the shepherd. "I appreciate you bringing her back," she said, unable to put any warmth in her voice.

"I'm sorry I didn't bring her back earlier," said Rob, without a trace of regret in his voice, "but she and Tad were having such a good time that I didn't see any hurry, especially when I had work to do in the fields."

"Thank you for bringing her anyway," Cathie repeated, feeling the hint was broad enough for anyone to see that she was anxious for Rob to be gone.

"Not at all," he replied blandly, his brown eyes mocking the coolness of her expression. His gaze flicked to the glistening curls of her shoulder length hair. "I'm glad to see that your hair didn't suffer from the cockleburs."

"Cockleburs? What's this about the cockleburs?" Clay picked up the subject immediately, despite the glaring look from Cathie.

"Didn't she tell you?" Rob looked innocently at Clay. "Cathie took a header into some itchweed and cockleburs when she was out to the farm yesterday. It took a while for me to get the burrs out of her hair and clothes."

If looks could kill, Cathie would have sent Rob six feet under. She bit at her lower lip to keep the scathing retort from slipping out, aware that under the tan, her cheeks were taking on a rosy hue.

"No, she didn't mention it to me." Without looking, Cathie could feel the inquisitive eyes of her fiancé turn on her.

"It was hardly important," she shrugged.

"Oh, it could have been." A mocking smile curled one corner of Rob's mouth. "Especially if that beautiful honey-colored hair of yours had had to be cut to free it from the burrs." He glanced from one to the other. "You two are obviously going out somewhere, so I won't keep you any longer. I just wanted to return your dog."

After Rob had driven away, Cathie wasted no time in chaining the unhappy shepherd to her kennel. Andy winked at her broadly as Cathie walked past her to Clay.

"What was all that about?" Clay inquired when they were both in his car and en route to the theater.

"What?" Cathie asked, deliberately playing ignorant.

"That episode yesterday with Douglas."

"Just what he said. I tumbled into some weeds and got a few cockleburs in my clothes and hair."

Clay turned his attention away from the road

ahead of them to survey her with a particularly amused look. "It didn't sound quite as simple as that the way he told it."

"You can't go by what he said," she declared sharply.

"Why not?"

"Don't be silly, Clay. It's not worth arguing about," she insisted.

"Who's arguing?" Clay asked. After one more thoughtful glance, the subject was dropped ... to Cathie's relief.

CHAPTER SEVEN

A SATISFIED GLEAM lit her jade eyes as Cathie fluffed the short curls on top of her head. She hadn't realized how hot and heavy her long hair had been in the summer's heat. The small rectangular mirror in the choir's changing room confirmed the compliments she had received from her friends that the new, shorter style was attractive. What she couldn't see for herself was that the long hair had emphasized her youth while the perfectly-shaped shorter style of gently waving curls made her appear more womanly and alluring.

Clay, who often got upset with her but never angry, had been on the verge of it the night before when he had picked her up for their regular Saturday date. Cathie had always known he was old-fashioned and had more than once stated his preference for long hair, but she never dreamed he would attempt to dictate how she wore her own hair. It had been a totally unpleasant evening.

In all honesty, Cathie knew she hadn't been indulging in a mere whim when she had gotten her hair cut. The original decision had come from a defiant desire to show Rob Douglas that his compliments meant nothing to her. If he liked her hair long, then she disliked it. Clay might have put the wrong conjecture on such reasoning, so she hadn't confided in him.

It had been a disappointment in church this morning to discover that Rob Douglas wasn't in his usual pew. She would have enjoyed seeing the expression on his face when he saw her cropped-off hair. That moment of satisfaction would have to come another time, Cathie decided, smoothing her simply-styled, jade-green dress.

She was one of the last to leave the choir room. Clay wouldn't be waiting for her this Sunday. He was visiting his parents, and after last night's near argument Cathie had decided not to go with him. She didn't know quite what she would do since she couldn't remember the last time she had spent a Sunday without Clay.

As she reached the pavement, she was toying with the idea of driving to Black Hawk Lake for an afternoon swim when she heard someone call her name. Cathie glanced back toward the church and saw Rob Douglas walking toward her. His lithe, athletic stride automatically called attention to him and she could feel the questioning eyes of the remaining members of the congregation turn toward her. Cathie could almost read their thoughts as she felt herself reddening that Rob Douglas had singled her out in front of everyone. They had probably all noticed the absence of Clay.

To make matters worse, Rob took her by the elbow and led her aside so they wouldn't be blocking the pavement, then retained the light grip on her arm. His eyes flicked over her hair and then alighted on her face.

"That's quite an improvement," he commented dryly.

"I thought you liked long hair," Cathie declared without thinking.

That half-smile curved his mouth as he looked down at her with lazy amusement. "I don't like long hair just for the sake of long hair. This style suits your personality a bit more. It's a little cheeky and sophisticated, very much like a feline."

This wasn't turning out the way she intended it at all. "What did you want to speak to me about?" she demanded, wanting a quick end to the conversation.

"I found a small trunk tucked away in the corner of the attic that must be your grandparents. It's filled with old clothing and such, from what I could tell. Since it's rather heavy, I thought if you could come out to my place this afternoon I could help you load it into your car and take it home."

Cathie had expected him to bring up something to do with Tad. She was at a loss for words when she discovered that he was only attempting to return something that quite evidently belonged to her family now.

"Yes, I can come out this afternoon," she replied, blinking up at him in confusion.

"Around three?" Rob asked with the complacency of a man who knows the answer is yes.

"I'll be there," Cathie nodded.

His hand left her elbow as he stepped away, raising his voice almost deliberately for the benefit of the onlookers to say, "I'll see you this afternoon, then."

Cathie's teeth ground tightly together as she saw the speculating looks appear in the men's eyes while the women regarded her with disapproval. How many times had she joked that in a small town something was no sooner done than said, but she had never thought she would be the object of the censure. They surely couldn't believe that she was arranging an assignation with Rob Douglas on the church lawn? Well, the damage was done, Cathie thought to herself, and idle talk never hurt anyone. If only that nagging feeling would leave that Rob Douglas had known all along that this was going to happen.

The short walk from the church to her house was completed in record time as anger lent impetus to her pace. Once there, Cathie debated whether to change into a pair of casual slacks and blouse before deciding that if she remained wearing the green dress and her open-toes white sandals with their high heels she would be less likely to be talked into staying by Tad or Rob.

Her original plans for the day called for eating her midday meal out and Cathie stuck to it, choosing a leisurely drive over the back roads of the farmland to pass the time before her appointment with Rob Douglas at the Homeplace. When her grandparents were alive they had spent many a pleasant hour doing the same thing. Her grandfather, even though no longer able to farm himself, was always interested in the condition of his neighbor's crops. Cathie could almost hear his comments as she drove past the neat, symmetrical fields of corn and wheat.

"Arthur has a good-looking field of soy beans there," or "That corn crop of MacDuff's is a disgrace. Just look at the weeds in the field!" Corn had been Grandfather Carlsen's favorite subject. He had always been extremely proud that Iowa was known as the "Tall Corn" state. Cathie smiled as she remembered how he used to tease her slightly plump grandmother that she had been corn bred and corn fed, just like the succulent Iowa beef.

A hen pheasant dashed across the road in front of her, forcing Cathie to slow down. Wavelike rows of young corn bordered each side of the road, freshly disced so that the rich, black soil contrasted sharply with the green of its stalk and leaves and the burgeoning tassels on top. When she had been a child, the measuring stick for a good corn crop—barring bad weather— had been if it was knee-high by the Fourth of July. With all the agricultural improvements that had been made, it was usually hip-high by that time.

As a meadowlark exposed his yellow throat to the sun from his perch on a fencepost and trilled his song to the country, Cathie arrived at another intersection in the graveled road. She made the turn, experiencing the desire of an old carriage horse to hurry the last mile home. There, on the small hilltop on the other side of the Boyer River, sat the farm buildings that until Rob Douglas came had always constituted the Homeplace.

The memories had closed around her and it was hard to bring herself back to the reality of a new owner without bringing resentment back, too. Ten minutes early, her gold watch told her as she made the turn off the county road on to the short lane. But it wasn't only resentment that was making her uneasy about this visit with Rob Douglas. There was something else that made her apprehensive to be around him that had nothing to do with his owning her grandparents' farm.

A strange car was parked in the driveway in front of the yard. As she drew closer, Cathie recognized the man behind the wheel as Charlie Smith's father. If it hadn't been that he had already seen her and was waving, she would have turned and driven right back out. *Stop feeling so guilty for coming out here,* she chided herself, parking the car a few feet away from his.

"Good afternoon, Mr. Smith," she called gaily as she stepped out of her car. The screen door banged at the house and Cathie glanced around to see Charlie and Tad walking down the path followed by Rob.

"How are you, Miss Carlsen," Charlie's father replied, tilting his straw hat back to reveal the white band around his forehead in contrast to his sunburned face. "Chuck and I were planning on doing a little fishing down at the river. We just stopped up here to make sure it was all right with Mr. Douglas."

"Hi, Miss Carlsen," Charlie greeted her before turning to his father to babble excitedly. "Tad knows a real good place to fish so I invited him along. He says we'll catch lots and lots."

"Come along, then, Tad," the man said, waving airily. "Grab your pole and climb in."

Tad glanced anxiously from Cathie to his father, his expression revealing that he was unsure whether to leave now that Cathie had arrived.

"Run along, Tad," Rob prompted gently. "Cathie only came out this time to pick up a trunk that was left behind in the moving."

After a quick "hello" in her direction, Tad dashed off for the garage and his bamboo pole. Cathie murmured a quiet greeting to Rob, letting her gaze slide away from the look of lazy amusement in his dark eyes. She stood silently by as Rob introduced himself to Ray Smith and listened to their brief exchanges about the weather and the crops until Tad came sprinting back with his pole in his hand.

Charlie urged him into the back seat of the car and Cathie found it hard to believe that Charlie had been the one to lead the rest of the class into chanting "tadpole." Although there was still a certain air of reserve around Tad as he sat next to Charlie, there was still the triumph of being able to show another boy where to catch fish which had an equalizing effect. Despite all Charlie's mischievousness, even to starting that horrible chant, Cathie knew there wasn't a malicious bone in his body. Everyone was his friend.

"Tad has been fishing every day since you were last here," Rob stated after the Smith car had left the driveway.

"Being with Charlie will do him good," Cathie commented. "That's one boy who's all boy. Tad will probably learn a lot that you'll regret."

"Snakes in the pocket and that sort of thing," Rob chuckled. The throaty sound was a pleasing accompaniment to the gentle rustle of the breeze in the cottonwoods. "I eagerly await that day."

Cathie didn't want to get into any discussion about his son. She was already too involved in their affairs, so she had to swallow back that shared feeling of victory that she and Rob had coaxed Tad out of his shell.

"I appreciate you letting me know about the trunk," she said, deftly changing the subject. "I can't imagine how mother and Aunt Dana missed it."

That knowing look came across his face and the small crescent scar near the one eye almost made it look as if he was winking at her inability to behave normally with him. But Rob smoothly slipped into the new conversation.

"The attic is very dimly lit and the trunk was in the far corner, so it's not inconceivable that they overlooked it. It's in the house," he said, stepping to the side so Cathie could precede him.

Her heart was skipping beats as she walked along the path to the house with Rob right behind her. His arm brushed hers as he opened the back door for her and followed her inside. Her sandals made a tapping sound on the linoleum steps up to the sun porch with the more solid sound of Rob's shoes right behind her. She hesitated at the top, glancing around for some sign of the trunk and, more importantly, the reassuring presence of a third person, namely Mrs. Carver.

"I left the trunk upstairs," said Rob, walking ahead of her to open the almost full-length door leading into the living room. "I thought you might want to go through it. As I said, there seemed to be mostly old clothes on top and I have a box of Tad's clothes I was going to give to the Salvation Army. You would be welcome to include whatever you didn't want to keep in with it." A crooked smile was tossed over his shoulder. "That way the trunk wouldn't be quite so heavy to carry down the stairs."

"Where's Mrs. Carver?" she asked.

"Visiting her daughter," Rob replied.

Cathie just wanted to take the trunk and run, then chided herself for being so cowardly. So she didn't trust Rob? Apart from the way he so arrogantly mocked her sometimes, there was no reason to feel that way. And she was quite able to take care of herself. Besides, there was that glint of amusement in his eyes that said he knew very well that she didn't want to spend an extra minute in his company. Her blond head tilted back defiantly as she gazed coolly at the brown head leading the way. She would show him that she was totally immune to his supposedly irresistible charms.

Cathie paused in the living room, ignoring Rob, who had reached the door leading to the stairwell. Her green eyes glanced around the room, taking in the large hooked rug that covered the floor and the comfortable Early American furniture in warm yellows and browns with a sprinkling of persimmon for color. It filled the room with old-fashioned ease and down-home warmth. She spitefully wished that the room would have been redone in those ugly modernistic furnishings that she disliked instead of this style that fitted so well into the simple farmhouse.

"Well?" Rob said softly from the stair door. "Do you find any drastic changes?"

"It's very nice," she said grudgingly. Her gaze trailed around the room again, stopping at the partially opened double doors that led into the parlor. The slight opening revealed unfinished wood shelving on a wall that had always been bare. "Are you remodeling the parlor?" Without waiting for an invitation, Cathie walked to the walnut-stained doors and pushed them open.

The parlor, that lovely old-fashioned room that had always sprung to life at Christmas time when a huge evergreen tickled the ceiling and brightly wrapped presents tumbled all over the floor, was no longer. Rows of shelves filled the entire north wall of the room, framing the large window in the center. The mint-green paint of the rest of the walls had been covered by rich walnut paneling. The floor space in between was a jumble of boxes and crates. Two over-stuffed chairs were draped with white sheets that still had fragments of sawdust clinging to the cotton cloth.

A typewriter stand stood in one corner, an iron-gray cover protecting the typewriter, and beside it was a desk cluttered with papers and books. Somehow, in the middle of the mess, was a long cylindrical roll of carpeting waiting patiently for the floor to be cleared so it could take its place. A vibrant dark gold color peeped from the ends as tufts of thick pile shag escaped the roll.

"I suppose it's somewhat of an understatement to say that the room is a mess right now," Rob commented in a complacent tone from his place behind her left shoulder. "Mrs. Carver swears it will be autumn before I ever get it done."

"Are you making this your . . . ." Cathie glanced around the partially redecorated room, wanting to feel resentment for the destruction of the parlor and all its old memories, but her mind's eye was visualizing the room as it would appear in its completed state. She knew it would be a room she would like. "Are you making this your office?" she finished.

"Office, den, study, whatever."

She could feel his shrug of indifference at placing a label on the room. A package of books rested on top of a large box, partially opened with two books sticking out. Their vividly colored jackets attracted her and Cathie stepped over to pick one up. The name Robert Douglas leaped at her where the author's name was written. Her startled expression turned to Rob.

"Are you a writer?" she gasped. The question itself was almost an insult since she was holding one of his books in her hands.

"Is that an accusation or a question?" Laughter danced from his eyes at her chagrin.

The discovery had caught her off guard as Cathie fumbled around for the words to cover her confusion. "I didn't mean it to sound like that. I just didn't know . . . . No one has ever mentioned that you wrote books."

"Now my secret is out. Or at least, you hold it in your hands."

"Is it a secret?" Her jade-green eyes rushed to his face, trying to read the impenetrable expression that mocked her so openly.

"Since I don't use a pseudonym when I write, I don't see how it could be," he replied calmly, turning his attention from her to survey the room.

"Then why doesn't anyone know?" she asked, puzzled by this suggestion of modesty that didn't fit in at all with her conception of him.

"It didn't seem necessary to broadcast it to the world. I write mystery thrillers meant solely for the reader's entertainment and not any thought-provoking best-sellers designed to gain fame and fortune." Rob turned back to her, his gaze racing over her face with penetrating thoroughness. "Which doesn't mean I'm ashamed of what I write. I'm fairly good and enjoy myself while I'm working, but I don't believe I have false beliefs in my own importance."

Cathie glanced down at the book and opened the cover. The inside leaf contained a list of other books by Robert Douglas. "Why are you here? Working in the fields and remodeling rooms when you could be writing?"

"I told you the truth when I said that I had moved here to Iowa for Tad's benefit. I know you'll find it hard to believe, but I was brought up on a farm and I remember vividly the many pleasurable hours I spent roaming the country-

side, taking part in the planting and harvesting."
The surprised expression on Cathie's face drew
an open laugh from Rob. "What's the matter,
don't I look like your typical farm product
because I don't have a band of white on my
forehead where my hat sits?"

"We were told you were from Long Island,
New York. How could any of us know that you
might have been brought up on a farm?" she
defended herself.

"So what did you do?" he asked, with mocking emphasis on the "you." "Did you brand me
as a playboy, an adventurer?"

"I had no idea what you did for a living," she
replied, avoiding a direct answer. "Are you still
going to·write?"

"Of course," he nodded. "I have the evenings
in the summer and the long winters here will
give me quite a few free hours. Writing and
farming will blend well together, with just about
the same amount of satisfaction." Rob inclined
his head toward her in mock deference. "Now, if
I've satisfied the 'cat's' curiosity, would you like
to see the trunk?"

"I wasn't trying to pry in your private life,"
Cathie retorted, drawing herself up to her full
height which still left her several inches shorter
than Rob.

"Of course not, you were just curious," he
agreed smoothly, leading her again into the living room and to the stairwell door.

Cathie held tightly to the smooth banister
railing of the el-shaped stairs, her nervousness
increasing with each step. All her preconceived

ideas of Rob were being eliminated one by one. She preferred thinking of him as an egotistical Easterner, far removed from rural community life. It made him easier to dislike.

"Tad has the room at the head of the stairs and Mrs. Carver sleeps in the bedroom over the kitchen," Rob spoke, climbing the steps ahead of Cathie. "The middle bedroom is so large I don't know what we'll ever use it for, since I'm using the large bedroom off the study downstairs."

"My grandparents intended to have a large family when they built the house, but there ended up being only three." Cathie felt the need to explain the reason for the spacious upstairs. "There were always plenty of relatives to keep it filled, though."

The middle room was virtually empty with only a few boxes sitting around and the trunk that had brought Cathie here. It was difficult to step into the room and not expect to see the large four-poster bed on one side of the room and the single feather bed where she had slept as a child or the picture on the wall of a shepherd boy guarding his flock by moonlight. Before the memories crowded too close around her, Cathie walked quickly toward the trunk, opening the lid to lift out the men's clothing packed on top. The gentle scent of lavender clung to the tweeds and wools.

"Here's the box I was putting Tad's old clothes in," said Rob, carrying a cardboard box over to the trunk where Cathie was kneeling.

"Thank you," she murmured absently, placing the clothes in the box knowing they would be of no use to her.

Below the men's clothing was a horsehair blanket. With a gasp of happy surprise, Cathie shook it open, running her hand over the silken fineness of the dark brown and white spotted hide.

"I remember this!" She turned excitedly to Rob. "It's the hide from Uncle Andrew's horse, Pal. When the horse died, he sent the hide off to a tanner in Minnesota to make a blanket out of it. In the old days, they used them as buggy blankets. When I was a little girl, Grandma used to let me put it on my bed."

"Then I'm glad I found the trunk." Rob watched lazily as she fingered the green velvet material on the reverse side of the blanket.

Cathie lovingly folded the blanket and set it to the side, turning to the layers of tissue in the trunk. As she carefully lifted them away, her hands touched satiny material.

"It's grandmother's wedding dress," she breathed, very gently pushing away the tissue and holding the ivory and lace dress up. Her grandmother had been several inches shorter than Cathie and was quite small as a young girl, judging by the tiny waist of the dress. "I wish I were that small," she grinned. "I would wear it for my own wedding."

"Have you set the date, then?" Rob asked, his gaze flickering from the dress to her.

"No, not yet." Cathie shook her head, arranging the dress back in the bottom of the trunk surrounded by the protecting layers of tissue.

There was something in the way that he asked the question that put her on the defensive.

"You and Clay grew up together. Did you know all along you were in love with him, or did you just discover it all of a sudden?" His head was tilted inquiringly to one side as he studied her.

"I knew when I was in high school, but Clay discovered it when I followed him into college." Her reply sprang easily to her lips. It was a carbon copy answer to similar questions that friends and relatives had asked over the years.

"How long have you been engaged?"

Cathie touched the cluster of small diamonds that adorned the ring on her finger. "Clay gave me my ring after he passed his bar exams a year ago."

"And you aren't married yet." The movement of his brown head echoed the mocking disbelief in his voice. "What are you waiting for?"

"We're trying to find a house we like. As soon as we do, we'll get married."

"For two people who are as in love as you profess to be, you're both exhibiting an admirable amount of patience." Humor etched itself in the tanned lines around his eyes and mouth.

"Why?" A trace of temper added a sharpness to her words. "Because we're being practical? Because we didn't dash to the altar the minute we decided we were in love? Just because we had the good sense to wait until Clay could get himself established in a good law practice and we could find a nice home to live in isn't a reason to doubt the way we feel toward each other."

"Haven't you ever experienced any urgent desire or need to be married?" The sharpness of his gaze refused to allow her to look away.

It took Cathie a full second to understand the point of his carefully worded question. Her back stiffened. "You're confusing lust with love. They aren't the same thing at all."

"I wouldn't begin to argue that they are." The daggers she flashed at him couldn't find any opening in his smooth and mocking countenance. "But there is a physical desire that accompanies love which is part of the reason two people get married."

"Well, our love is based on friendship and companionship. This physical aspect that you keep emphasizing comes quite far down on our list of reasons to get married," Cathie declared icily.

"Did you ever date anyone other than Clay?"

"Of course," she said huffily, closing the trunk and securing the latches. "I went out with several other men before I was engaged."

"Did you kiss them?"

"Yes, I kissed them," she answered in a tight voice of barely repressed anger. "This conversation is ridiculous. None of this is any of your business."

"I never said it was," Rob shrugged. "I was just curious how an attractive woman like you could remain so unmoved by one of the pleasanter and more satisfying aspects of being in love. It crossed my mind that maybe you'd never been properly made love to."

"Kissing is grossly overrated," she snapped,

now knowing how prudishly sure of herself she sounded. "It's pleasant and enjoyable, but there's certainly no heart-pounding or earth-shaking revelations, as those romance books lead you to believe."

There was a fluttering like butterfly wings in her stomach as Rob appeared suddenly closer to her, although he hadn't moved. A glitter of mischief lit up the depths of his velvet eyes as his gaze settled on her mouth. Cathie moistened her lips nervously, then swallowed, conscious of the trip-hammer beat of her heart.

"There's some truth to that," he agreed blandly. "Would you object to testing your theory?"

"How?" Cathie demanded, eyeing him with marked distrust.

"By kissing me."

His calm statement jolted her. "I will not!" She retorted indignantly. "How could you even suggest such a thing?"

She moved to step past him, but the mockery in his expression halted her. "Probably because I knew you wouldn't do it," said Rob, lowering his voice to a jeering taunt. "You haven't got the nerve to really kiss me."

Angry words of biting denial formed on her lips until she intuitively realized that that was exactly what Rob was expecting. She would show him! A falsely sweet smile put a sugar coating on her pink tinted lips. Then instead of stepping past him as she had intended to do, she stepped toward him. Cool jade-green eyes stared up into the amused brown ones. Her hands rested lightly on his chest to balance as she raised herself on tiptoes to reach the sensuous line of his mouth.

CHAPTER EIGHT

CATHIE'S LEGS WERE TREMBLING as she drew closer to the smooth, close-shaven face, the delicate lingering scent of lavender from the trunk mingling with the potently intoxicating aroma of masculine cologne that clung to Rob's tanned cheeks. An electric tingling vibrated through her at the joining of his lips against hers. His mouth was warm and mobile, persuading but with a firmness that demanded and received a response.

Cathie had a strange feeling of unreality, of being slowly sucked into a dangerous pool of quicksand without a single attempt to save herself. She was being pulled down, down. . . . His strong arms circled her waist and drew her against the burning warmth of his muscular chest, arching her to the thrust of his hard body. Cathie found herself totally surrendering to this embrace that was half heaven and half hell. Her hands moved to the back of his neck, letting the hair curl over her fingers while she molded herself closer to his outline. Rob's kiss was consuming her, wholly and completely, dragging out the last vestiges of resentment and inhibitions, making her aware of the true differences of the sexes and what making love meant.

Then slowly there was a disentangling of their

lips and Cathie was being gently set away, her
feet seeming to be placed on solid ground, free
of the treacherous depths of the quicksand
embrace. Her blood was singing a wild song of
ecatasy in her ears as she fought to bring her
breathing to a regular rate. Her eyelids fluttered
open, revealing shimmering pools of green
reflecting the disturbance Rob had caused. Her
gaze eagerly examined his face to see if he had
been as moved as she, but there was only the
slightest irregular beat in the vein running near
his temple.

"Sometimes it can be like that between two
people," Rob said calmly.

He had just turned her world upside down,
made all her firmly held beliefs vanish with one
fiery kiss, and he was acting as if it was the most
natural statement to make. She had never felt
this drowning sensation when Clay kissed her,
only a tender, loving desire to give and receive.
There was no overwhelming reaction between
them such as she had just experienced with Rob.

But with Clay there was that precious feeling
of security, Cathie argued silently with herself.
She wasn't drawn to the brink and then plummeted into some whirlpool of passionate long-
ing. The first emotion would last forever. How
long would the second last, she asked herself
and shuddered inwardly at the frightening
thought. She mustn't allow herself to fall in love
with Rob Douglas, to be caught up in the spell
he was trying to weave.

His dark eyes were still regarding her, waiting
for her to comment, to admit that it hadn't been

a casual kiss. A glittering light of anger flamed in her eyes as she studied the tall, arrogant man standing so calmly in front of her. Rob Douglas, the new owner of the Carlsen farm—the Homeplace that was so precious to her and had always been so much a part of her life. He was living here now where he had no right to be, regardless of any signatures on legal documents. His presence had already destroyed one long-held dream of hers to live on the farm and raise her family. She wasn't about to let him destroy her relationship with Clay. For nearly six years she had planned to marry Clay and she was not going to allow one kiss from this usurper to change her mind.

"Did you expect me to melt into a quivering mass of jelly at your feet?" Cathie asked scornfully, tilting her head back so he could see the contempt written in her face. "I concede that you're quite skilled in evoking a response from a woman, but the effect doesn't last."

Her scathing words only brought a sparkle of indulgent amusement to his eyes. "I have half a mind to make you eat that pride of yours," Rob grinned without the slightest dent to his ego.

He moved toward her and Cathie took a quick step backward, tripping over the trunk and nearly falling. His quick reaction kept her upright although the touch of his hands on her back sent fresh goosebumps up her spine. Rob knew it, knew that part of her wanted to taste the wild honey of temptation again.

"Let me go!" she ordered, surprised at how convincing her voice sounded with his mouth so hypnotically close.

She expected him to disregard her demand and force her to submit to another embrace. She had to hide her surprise and regret when Rob did as she asked and let her go.

"You can sheathe your claws, Cat," he smiled. "Patience is one of a writer's most valuable virtues. I've learned that waiting only increases the pleasure."

The fuse to Cathie's temper took fire and raced away. "Then you'd better pray for a major catastrophe, Mr. Douglas," she exploded, "because I wouldn't look at you unless you were the last man on earth, and even then I would probably still get violently ill at the sight of you!"

"Illness!" He laughed outright at that, like an adult at a child's spiteful words. "Is that the way you're reasoning away that funny feeling at the pit of your stomach? Oh, my little green-eyed Cat, you have a great deal to learn."

"You won't be teaching me," she said determinedly, trying to ignore the twisted knots in her stomach.

Rob sighed almost contentedly as he finally turned his diamond-bright gaze from her. "I know you're anxious to run away. Would you like me to carry the trunk down to the car for you?"

The trunk? Cathie touched her forehead, feeling the short blond curls trumbling about her head in disarray. That was why she had come here in the first place—for the trunk. That seemed an eternity ago.

"Yes, please," she said stiffly, watching with grudging admiration as he picked up the heavy old trunk with ease and carried it through the door toward the stairwell.

After the trunk had been safely stowed in the back of the car, Rob turned toward Cathie, her car keys still in his hand. She reached out to take them, but his fingers closed over them.

"I can't let you leave without offering you something cold to drink," he said. At the expression of refusal leaping into her face, Rob continued before she could voice it. "We could sit over there underneath that big walnut tree by the cornfield. If you don't feel like carrying on a civil conversation, we can sit and listen to the corn grow."

Cathie inhaled sharply at his last statement. She couldn't count the times she had heard her grandfather make the same comment. The walnut tree had been his choice, too, for those lazy summer evenings when even the crickets' and cicadas' songs were slow and somnolent. Often Cathie had sat with her grandfather and listened to those soft crackling sounds which he had assured her was the corn growing in the nearby field. And now this intruder was saying the same thing, not laughingly as Clay had always done, but sincerely like her grandfather.

"No," she breathed quickly, her eyes widening as her blond head made a negative movement. "No, I don't care for anything. I have to go."

"Tad will be sorry he missed you," said Rob. His gaze narrowed, not guessing how close his casual comment had come to piercing her shield of angry pride, but knowing for a moment she had been vulnerable to his suggestion.

"Yes, well," Cathie stumbled, "he knows there'll be other times. May I have my keys?"

Rob handed them over to her and she slid quickly behind the wheel of her car before some traitorous part of her would agree to stay. As she drove out the lane, Cathie made a silent promise to herself that she would begin breaking off her connection with Tad. It would have to be done slowly so he wouldn't feel she was deserting him, but if his afternoon fishing expedition with Charlie was successful it wouldn't be too difficult to accomplish. The sooner she avoided all contact with the Douglas family the better off she would be.

This conclusion was reached by Cathie's grim determination that she never wanted to be trapped in a situation like today where she was tricked into kissing Rob Douglas. Never again did she want to lose control of her emotions and be swept away on a rising tide of pointless desires. Her mind reached the decision with cool and calm calculations, which made the tears on her cheeks come as a surprise when their salty taste reached her lips.

THERE WAS THE WHOOSH of another rocket leaping into the midnight-blue sky, then a sudden explosion of color drawing sighing "ahs" from the crowd gathered around the open athletic field. Tiers of artificial stars in layers of red, green and blue gently fell toward the earth as another rocket made its ascent. Cascading spirals of glittering gold whistled their way down to make room for more gaily colored shooting stars. Elsewhere around the fields was the rat-a-tat of a string of firecrackers being set off to accompany the more spectacular fireworks display.

The Fourth of July—Independence Day—was marked all over the country by traditional celebrations such as the one Cathie was now watching, where the shattering, vibrating boom of the cannon rockets was softened by scattering showers of makebelieve stars. And Cathie still felt the same mixture of awe and excitement as she had when she was a child. The spasmodic illumination of the sky revealed the memories of past happiness in her eyes when her gaze was drawn to a pair of young children waving their magic wands called sparklers. They were dancing on the blanket their parents, like Cathie and Clay, had spread on the ground.

Another group of children was racing around the parked cars. Cathie recognized Charlie Smith as the leader and was surprised to see Tad among the pack. She glanced furtively around for his father to find him quietly studying her several yards away. Rob Douglas was leaning against a car parked beside Clay's with several other people, one of whom was Connie. His head dipped in a silent greeting to her and Cathie spun around to concentrate on the fireworks display, feeling a burning heat rush over her cheeks.

She had been so successful at avoiding any contact with Rob the past two weeks that she had truly believed her luck would last. She might have known he would bring Tad here tonight to see the fireworks, but Cathie had been confident that the secluded corner of the field where she and Clay were would be off the beaten track.

"Hello." Rob's voice came from Clay's side of the blanket. "Do you mind if we put our blanket next to yours, Clay?"

"Help yourself," Clay smiled. "The ground is free."

"Hi, Clay. Hi, Cathie," Andy declared pertly, forcing Cathie to turn in Rob's direction in order to greet her roommate.

It wasn't just Rob and Connie as she had first thought but Andy and three others. The fair-haired man she knew because she had met him at the house when he had come to pick Andy up for a date. The third girl was a nurse a few years older than Cathie and the man with her was a new vet who had just moved into the area. There was a brief flurry of introductions to make sure everybody knew everybody.

"It sure is hot tonight, isn't it?" Andy commented once the group was settled on the blankets with Andy and Rob spilling over onto Cathie's and Clay's—at Clay's suggestion. "The temperature must still be in the nineties and it's so humid," she continued, adding stress to the last word. "Don't you just feel sticky all over, Cathie?"

"It is uncomfortable," Cathie agreed, keeping herself well back in Clay's shadow to conceal herself from Rob's eyes.

"What an understatement!" Andy exclaimed. "All I do is move my arm and I sweat like a horse!"

"Do you remember what your grandmother always used to say?" Clay tilted his head toward Cathie with a confiding look.

"How could I forget?" she replied, widening her eyes in agreement. "I'll have you know, Andy, that horses sweat, men perspire, and ladies glow. At least, according to my grandmother they did."

"Well, I am glowing!" Andy announced firmly, drawing chuckles from the small group.

Before the subject could be carried further, Tad catapulted himself into the group, followed by a panting Charlie Smith. His cheeks were flushed and his sandy-brown hair clung to the perspiration on his forehead. Tad looked like a typical boy, grinning and excited.

"Charlie asked me if I could stay overnight with him," he said breathlessly to Rob. "Can I, please?" His bright hazel eyes darted over to Cathie. "Hi!"

"Hello, Tad," she smiled, happiness filling her heart at the genuine warmth in his eyes. No matter how she felt about his father she couldn't hold anything back in her affection for his son.

"Do your parents know about your invitation, Charlie?" Rob inquired, turning from the eager face of his son to the shifting, impatient boy anxious to be away from the constricting adults.

"Yes, sir." The freckled face bobbed quickly. "I've got six brothers and sisters and my mom said another boy for one night wouldn't make any difference. Can he come? He can wear some of my clothes and pajamas."

"Please," Tad inserted when Rob still hesitated to give his approval.

Andy's friend Dennis had engaged Clay in a conversation which left Cathie free to listen in on this exchange between father and son. Tad was joining in, becoming a part of other children his own age. Her jewel eyes gleamed with the success of his transition while she waited breathlessly in case Rob wouldn't agree. Rob must have sensed her anxious gaze resting on him. As he turned, his eyes silently asked her opinion. Her blond curls moved in a barely perceptible nod of agreement, and the velvet-brown eyes smiled back before Rob turned away.

"You can stay overnight, but—" the qualifying word halted the two boys in midflight "—I want you to take me to your parents, Charlie, so I can make arrangements to pick Tad up tomorrow when it's convenient for them."

Cathie watched the trio walk away, Rob's supple stride keeping pace with the two boys trotting hurriedly ahead of him. Some part of her was walking with him because of that strange, intimate look they had exchanged—a look that Cathie would rather forget, but its warmth was too fresh. Instead she turned to Clay, seeking his closeness to overshadow Rob's.

"Don't you think this fireworks display is better than last year's?" Cathie asked as another golden shower of swirling spirals drifted downward.

"You sound just like my aunt," Andy laughed before Clay could reply. "She says the same thing every year."

"You know Cathie is just a small-town girl,"

Clay said to Andy in a definitely teasing tone. "The Fourth of July is the most exciting evening in her life outside of Christmas."

"That doesn't speak very highly of you as my escort," Cathie retorted with impish humor, glad of the light-hearted conversation that diverted her thoughts from Rob.

"Oh, look!" Andy exclaimed, her dark head directing their attention to the fireworks. "They're lighting the flag. That means the end to the fireworks for this year."

All eyes turned to the large rectangular framework at the far end of the field. Like falling dominoes, the spark raced along the frame touching off white stripes, then red stripes, the field of blue and finally the stars. It was the finale, the close of the Fourth of July celebration until next year. As the flag display began spluttering out, the general exodus from the athletics field began.

"Let's wait until the crowd clears out," Clay suggested. "It's cooler sitting here in the open than being stuck in the car waiting on traffic."

In mute agreement the small group remained sprawled on their Indian blankets, chattering idly until Andy popped to her feet. "I know what let's do," she declared. "Let's all go to Black Hawk Lake and swim. It's a perfect night for it."

"Sure," Dennis joined in. "My folks have a cabin there. We can have something to drink and everything. They won't mind."

While the others were voicing their approval, Clay glanced at Cathie and quietly asked her opinion, "What do you think? Do you want to go?"

"If the water were in front of me right now," she sighed, "I would probably go jump in it with my clothes on. It feels hotter now than when the sun was up."

There was a flurry of voices as arrangements were made for swimming clothes to be picked up and a meeting place agreed on. In less than half an hour they were all back at the athletics field, the chosen meeting ground, with their swimming suits, towels and robes. But another member had joined their party, and Cathie felt a pinprick of doubt about the excursion as she gazed at Rob Douglas.

Andy was standing next to her as the men debated whether to drive their own cars or ride together in just two. "Is he going with us?" Cathie asked, keeping her voice low so it wouldn't carry.

"Who?" Andy's dark brows knitted together.

"Rob Douglas."

"Yes." A blank expression of surprise covered Andy's face at Cathie's unexpected question. "You don't have any objections, do you? As often as you have gone out to the farm to see him, you couldn't possibly still dislike the man. All the gossips in town are talking about it."

"I went out to the farm to see Tad, not his father." A decidedly defensive note crept into her voice. "I couldn't care less whether he goes with us or not," Cathie lied, knowing she would be self-consciously aware of him. "He just wasn't here when we made the arrangements."

"He came back later, I guess," Andy shrugged. "And you know Connie is still trying to get her hooks into him, so she was bound to invite him along. He doesn't seem too keen on her, though, not that I blame him. Outside of being beautiful, what has she got that I haven't? I wish I were a teacher like you, then I could talk to Rob about his son like you do. He might notice me then."

Cathie was saved from commenting by Clay walking toward her. "We decided to each drive our own car," he told her. That was welcome news since she had been dreading the prospect of Rob and perhaps Connie riding with them.

As the gathering broke up to get into their respective cars, Cathie couldn't keep her eyes from straying to Rob, only to color furiously when he glanced her way and nodded, the knowing light in his eyes mocking her irritation. Dennis and Andy led the small caravan in his car while Cathie and Clay brought up the rear. They rode in silence for several miles.

"What are you so quiet about?" Clay finally asked, his hazel eyes turning their gaze from the road long enough to glance at Cathie. Her head was turned away from him so he could only see her honey-colored hair.

"I have a slight headache," she said, touching her temple to emphasize her words. "I don't know that I really feel like going swimming."

"It's probably the heat," Clay said, brushing aside the problem. "Once you get in the water and cool off you'll feel better."

"I doubt it," she replied caustically, directing

her spite at Clay since Rob wasn't there. "With everybody splashing and yelling, it will probably get worse."

"What's the matter with you lately?" Clay demanded. "You're constantly changing your mind. Two weeks ago you wouldn't go with me to visit my parents because you were singing in the choir at church. Then last Sunday, you took off to visit your parents. Earlier tonight you could hardly wait to go swimming, and now, not even an hour later, you don't want to go. This isn't like you, Cathie."

How could she begin to explain to Clay what the source of her real problem was? How could she tell him that she wanted to avoid any contact with Rob Douglas? It was something she couldn't even explain to herself, except that ever since he came to this town, her world had been changing. Nothing was the same as it used to be as much as she tried to make it so. The slight drumming in her temples wasn't bothering her as much as the building tension at spending time with Rob Douglas.

Cathie rubbed the back of her neck and stared into the black curtain of night outside the car windows. "I don't know why I'm so moody lately," she murmured, drawing a deep breath. "But you're probably right. Once I get in the water, my headache will more than likely go away."

What else could she say? Any more protests about going swimming would have meant more questions, and if Clay asked more questions, he might just find out the truth. Besides it was silly,

Cathie told herself, to let the presence of Rob dampen her evening.

CHAPTER NINE

"OOHH, THE WATER IS COLD!" Connie said shivering, her feet dancing away from the gentle waves that lapped along the sandy shore.

"No, it's not," Andy called from where she was treading water. "It's really warm once you get in it."

"Come on." Clay grabbed Connie's arm and pulled her into the lake, laughing at her shrieks of displeasure as he firmly immersed her in the water.

Cathie needed no promptings as she waded into the cool water until it was nearly touching her white bikini, then submerged to swim toward the raft anchored several yards from shore. Through water-spiked lashes, she saw Clay swimming beside her, his grin challenging her to a race. He was already lifting himself onto the raft when she reached it. The rest of the group had gathered there too, with the exception of Connie and Dennis. But it was Rob's hands and not Clay's that reached down to help Cathie onto the floating platform.

Under the glow of the moonlight, his tanned body glistened like a bronzed statue, muscular and smooth, naked except for his black trunks. She kept her eyes averted from his face, feeling an attack of breathlessness that had no basis in exercise overtake her as she inadvertently glanced at him, her senses traitorously ignited at his touch. The second her balance was established she eluded the firm but not restraining grasp of his hands and moved away toward Clay, her only refuge from the magnetic pull Rob's nearness produced.

"Rob, give me a hand up," Connie called imperiously from the water near the raft. Cathie was thankful to have the attention diverted from her; she needed the time to regain her composure.

Dennis came drifting past the raft, lolling in an oversized rubber tire while propelling himself with his hands. A duplicate of the tire was floating a few feet behind him along with a pair of yellow air mattresses. There was a scramble from the raft into the water to see who could lay claim to the floating objects which ended in laughs and shrieks as one swimmer after another was capsized by the rest. Cathie joined, finding safety in numbers.

It was several minutes later while the others were engrossed in their water game of king of the mountain that Cathie slipped away from the noisemakers, taking one of the forgotten air mattresses. There was too much body contact in that game, and Cathie knew that sooner or later it would include her and Rob. Agilely she slipped onto the mattress, reclining on her back as the gentle rocking motion of the water carried her quietly away from the robust crowd.

The smiling face of a silver-dollar moon illuminated the lake, chasing the dark shadows away to hide under the trees that gathered near the shore. It was peaceful lying here on this soft cradle, Cathie thought, relaxing as the waves carried her farther from the group and closer to the shore.

There was no sound or movement to betray the presence of another person, but all of a sudden Rob's head appeared beside her. His brown hair, curling and wet around his forehead, gave him a rakish look to match the fiery blaze in his eyes.

"What are you doing so far away from the rest of us?" An eyebrow arched over the brilliant light in his eyes. "We're operating according to the buddy system tonight. There's to be no separation unless it's in pairs."

The initial shock was over and the blood was again starting to pump through her heart. "Where's Clay?" Cathie slid off the mattress into the water, using it as a shield against the penetrating gaze that had thoroughly raked her skimpily clad body.

"You cling to him as if he were a security blanket," Rob mocked. Like Cathie, he was using the natural buoyancy of the air mattress to keep him afloat without treading water. "What is it you're afraid of?"

"I'm not afraid of anything," she asserted, pushing her wet curls away from her face as she eyed him with false boldness.

His hand reached out and captured her arm, pulling her easily through the water to him. They had drifted close enough to shore so that Rob, because of his superior height, could touch bottom. Cathie could feel it just out of reach of her tiptoes. Without its support, struggling was wasted effort. He brought her close to him, his hands burning her flesh where they touched the nakedness of her waist. As he drew her tighter into the circle of his arms, Cathie tried to hold herself away, yet needing to cling to him to keep her head above water.

One of his hands moved to the back of her hair, holding her firmly while his head, framed against a star-spangled sky, began its slow descent. The feel of his sleek body pressed against hers was a potent sensation as the heat from him generated a different fire in Cathie. Shudders of sweet ecstasy quaked through her when his mouth closed over hers, expertly arousing the desire that she had always before kept suppressed. Rob was an irresistible force that she had to resist. It was a supreme test of will to keep her arms from encircling the hard smooth shoulders and mold herself closer to his body. In that Cathie succeeded, only to have her lips betray her and part under the sensually demanding and experienced request of his.

It was torturous bliss, wanting this kiss and despising herself for that want. It was Clay she was going to marry, not Rob. It was Clay who should be making her respond physically like this. When she thought she couldn't stand not giving herself wholeheartedly to the embrace, his mouth moved away from hers. Rob still held her tightly against him, his mouth moving softly against her golden hair. Cathie's head rested weakly against his shoulder, her breath silent sobs in her attempt to regain control. Shame and humiliation inflamed her because she had responded to a man who was not her fiancé. Yet she wanted to feel the hard pressure of his mouth on hers again.

"You're trembling like a frightened little cat," Rob murmured. "You're afraid, but you're afraid of the wrong thing."

Tears burned her eyes and she held them tightly shut. "Let me go!" she demanded in a tense voice that cried to be silenced by his lips.

"Is that what you want?"

"Yes." Hoarseness rasped her assertion.

As Rob let her drift away from him, he kept a steadying grip under her arms that loosened as she began treading water on her own. It was all she could do not to swim back to his open, inviting arms. Cathie glanced over her shoulder at the laughter and splashing horseplay of the rest of their party. She was suddenly cold, terribly cold and unwilling to face Clay as though nothing had happened. The darkness of the tree-lined beach beckoned and after casting Rob a condemning look, she struck out toward it, her arms cleaving the water with sharp, vigorous strokes.

Blinding hate enveloped her as she walked the last few yards to shore and strode toward the oversized blue beach towel she had left on the sand. At that moment Cathie hated Rob Douglas with a violent, sickening rush of emotion. The ache at the pit of her stomach told her that he was awakening her to the needs of the flesh as only her future husband should. Rob was changing her. Even Clay had noticed it. And she hated Rob for that, for disrupting her safe, secure world.

With hard, vigorous movements, Cathie scrubbed every clinging droplet of water from her skin, the harsh rubbing chastizing the weakness of her flesh. When the fury of her rage passed, she slung the towel around her shoulders and sunk to the ground in the darkness of an overhanging tree. Gazing out at the glacial moon and the brittle silver of the stars, she shivered, then caught a flash of yellow flame out of the corner of her eye.

"Here." Rob stood above her, his approach muted by the traitorous cushion of the sand, holding a cigarette toward her.

"I don't smoke," she said icily, but he pushed it into her hands anyway. It was something for her trembling hands to hold on to, so she kept it. He was obviously impervious to the coolness of the night as he lowered himself to the sand beside her, his naked chest glistening in the pale moonlight. "I didn't ask you to join me." The frigid sarcasm of her voice lashed out at him while she wished she could do the same with her hands.

A cloud of cigarette smoke hung in the air between them, as Rob lazily reclined on one arm. "I know you didn't," he replied with infuriating calm.

"Do you have any idea how much I despise you?" Cathie demanded, her green eyes shooting fiery sparks as she glared at him. "You are the most loathsome, disgusting man I've ever met! How could you be so brazenly uncivilized as to make love to a woman when the man she's engaged to is not twenty yards away?"

"Why didn't you call out to him to rescue you from my barbaric person?" he retorted smoothly, a glint of retaliatory anger in his dark eyes. Cathie's sharp intake of breath was an admission that he had found the vulnerable chink in her defensive armor. "You may call that an engagement ring, but it's nothing more than a friendship ring. You can't love him and kiss me like you just did."

"I'm going to marry Clay," Cathie declared, a hollow ring to her voice.

"Then I pity both of you."

"Pity?" She turned her puzzled, angry face toward him. "Why should you pity us?"

"I pity Clay more than I do you," said Rob, inhaling on his cigarette. "Because he'll end up with a dissatisfied unhappy wife and won't know why."

"And you do, I suppose." She turned away from him to study the granules of sand at her feet, his words cutting more deeply than she cared to admit.

"Yes. Would you like to know what's wrong with you?" he asked, an arrogant smile on his face.

Her mouth was compressed in a tight line. "Not particularly," she said with a dismissive shake of her head. "But I have the feeling you're going to tell me whether I ask you to or not."

Rob leaned forward and rested his arms on his knees as he contemplated her profile thoughtfully. "You haven't grown up yet, little kitten." He smiled as she gave him a startled look. Many things she could be accused of, but at that moment she was more aware of herself as a woman than she had ever been. "You're still living in some fantasy world that you built when you were a romantic teenager. You mapped everything out to enclose yourself into a cocoon of security. You chose Clay to marry because he was a link with your childhood happiness. With him, there would be no secrets or surprises because you'd grown up with him. But your plan included the farm where your idyllic marriage would be acted out. That's why you and Clay have kept finding excuses to keep from getting married, because you wanted the proper setting. My arrival disrupted your world before you even met me."

Cathie nodded numbly in agreement, uncaring of the glittering fire of satisfaction that lit his brown eyes. His words were so close to what had actually happened that it frightened her, casting doubts as to how genuine her affection for Clay really was and more doubts as to why she was marrying him.

"Tell me, Cat," Rob continued, "did you just ignore the physical aspect of a man-woman relationship or was it something you were going to endure in order to have the children who would one day discover all the magic of the farm? Why did you become a teacher? To maintain your connection with your childhood?"

His arrows of speculation were coming too fast for her to ward off. She cupped her hands over her ears so she wouldn't have to hear any more. "Stop it!" Cathie cried. "I don't want to hear any more of your stupid theories!"

With her eyes shut she didn't see his hands reach out to grasp hers and pull them away from her ears. At his touch, she struggled wildly until she had no more strength and submitted to the bruising hold he had on her wrists. But her eyes remained wide and rounded, reflecting the glittering anguish and fear that she would once again succumb to his charisma.

"I don't mean to hurt you." Rob's voice was low and soothing as if he were trying to calm a frightened animal. "There isn't anything wrong with having dreams or even trying to make them come true, unless it goes against your heart. Don't fight me any more, Cat, because of a dream."

The moonlight beamed down over his shoulder lighting her face and hiding Rob's face in its shadow. "I'm twenty-four years old," she protested weakly. "I'm not a child anymore. I know what I want."

She could see the flash of his teeth that signaled a smile, indulgent or mocking she couldn't tell. "There's always some part of all of us that remains a child."

"I love Clay." Cathie blinked at the tears hovering at the edge of her lashes, one last protest against her growing emotion for Rob. "I've always loved Clay."

"Of course you love him. But as a brother or a lover?"

"Why do you care?" There was a pleading,

protesting tone in her voice. "What difference could it possibly make to you?"

His hesitancy was a tangible thing. Unconsciously Cathie was holding her breath in wary anticipation of his reply. There was an overpowering feeling that his answer was of supreme importance, her future happiness hinged on it.

"I don't come into it at all, Cat." Rob finally spoke and her heart plummeted to her toes. He didn't care for her. "It's your relationship with Clay that's in question." He released her wrists and rolled to his feet to stand and look down at her. "Think over what I've said . . . for your own good."

The next instant he was several feet away, briskly toweling his wet hair. Cathie couldn't help watching him, studying the wide shoulders and the narrowing waist and hips. But the only thing she could feel was a lonely, aching emptiness somewhere in the region of her heart. She had told herself before that it would be foolish to fall in love with Rob. And she had finally done it.

"Cathie, what are you doing here?" Clay trotted out of the water, a happy grin of exhaustion on his face as he made his way toward her. He barely even glanced at Rob. "I wondered where you'd got to." As he walked past Rob, Cathie noticed the sharp contrast between Clay's almost white skin and the deep tan of Rob's. Clay collapsed on the sand beside Cathie, a wet arm playfully snatching her towel away. "You missed a lot of fun. What have you been doing, anyway?"

Cathie examined the clean lines of Clay's attractive face, not finding the strength and maturity that were etched so indelibly in Rob's face. "Rob and I were talking," she replied.

"Hashing poor Tad over again, huh? Or was he bringing you up to date on the changes at the Homeplace?" Clay grinned.

"No, actually we were just talking man to woman." Her statement didn't even bring a glimmer of surprise, much less jealousy, to Clay's face. He merely shrugged and began recounting how Connie's swimsuit top had accidentally came unhooked.

"Clay, I'm cold," Cathie interrupted impatiently. "Let's go home."

The rest of the party was just coming out of the water and Rob was walking to meet them. Connie had separated herself from the group to rush forward to meet him. And Cathie didn't like the twinge of pain that attacked her midsection at the burst of laughter from Connie at some unheard comment from Rob. Jealousy wasn't part of her nature, she had once bragged, but that was before Rob. She shivered.

"Say, you are a mass of goosebumps!" Clay exclaimed, running a dry but cool hand over her arm.

"I told you I was cold," Cathie snapped angrily, pulling the towel from his hands and wrapping it around her as she rose to her feet. Clay was forced to follow suit.

"Hey, where are you two going?" Andy called out as Cathie started toward the place where they had parked their cars.

"Cathie has an attack of chills. We're going to go ahead and leave now," Clay shouted back, lifting a hand in goodbye, but Cathie kept walking, not wanting to meet Rob's glance.

"Don't you want to stop and change clothes before we drive back?" Clay asked as Cathie slid into the passenger seat of his green compact car.

"I want to go home," she repeated determinedly.

"You don't have to be so touchy." He frowned as he slipped a blue cotton tee-shirt over his head and took his place behind the wheel. "I only thought that if you were cold you might feel better in some dry clothes."

After he had reversed the car out of the parking space and was on the road leading back to the highway, Cathie voiced the thought that had been uppermost in her mind. "Clay, would you like to get married? Right away, I mean."

"You mean not wait until we find a house? To simply get married on the spur of the moment, like that?" He snapped his fingers and gave Cathie a look that doubted her sanity. "That wouldn't make sense, to throw away all our plans."

"But what if it takes us another year to find the house we want?" she persisted, gazing straight ahead, her voice calm and unemotional.

"Then it takes another year," he replied, lifting his shoulders in a dismissive shrug.

"And after we find the house, it will take time to get it decorated and fixed the way we want it?"

"We've already talked all this out and figured

it into our plans." There was a bewildered frown on his forehead as he studied the pattern of his headlights on the concrete road.

"And after that, what kind of an excuse do you suppose we'll come up with to postpone the wedding?" Her eyes widened with false innocence as she turned them toward Clay.

"You aren't making any sense at all."

"What I think I'm asking is, do you really want to marry me, Clay?"

"Of course I do." There was a desperate note in Clay's confused voice as if he couldn't find the words to convince her. "Isn't that what we've been planning to do?"

Cathie sighed heavily, turning her troubled gaze away from him. "Planning and planning and planning, but never doing."

"Well, what do you want to do?" he demanded, half angrily. "Do you want to run off and elope tonight? Where would we live? I don't have enough cupboards in my apartment to hold my own clothes, let alone yours. You aren't suggesting that I move in with you, Connie and Andy, are you?"

"No, I'm not suggesting anything like that," she answered. Her shoulders sagged with the confusion of her own thoughts.

"Then explain to me what this conversation is all about," Clay sighed, his head moving from side to side in exasperation. Automatically he made the turn that would take him to Cathie's house. There was a moment of silence as he pulled into the driveway and turned off the engine. He turned sideways in his seat to study her.

"Clay, weren't you the least bit jealous when you found me with Rob?" Cathie had to swallow the lump in her throat before she could get that question out.

He cocked his head to the side, taken aback by her question and uncertain how to answer it. "Why should I have been jealous? You told me yourself that all you did was talk."

"He kissed me, too, Clay. And it wasn't the first time." The two bright spots of color on her cheeks didn't appear because she was embarrassed about telling him what had happened; they were there because of the way she had responded to those kisses. Her head lifted boldly to meet his gaze. There was surprise on his face, not anger or jealousy. "You aren't even upset now, Clay."

Inhaling deeply, he turned away to tap the steering wheel with his fingers, finding a lot of unanswered question in himself that suddenly needed answering. They were so close, Cathie thought to herself as she watched the silent soul-searching Clay was going through. She did love him deeply, but she knew that it was more the love of a sister or a friend.

"Have you fallen in love with Douglas?" Clay asked quietly.

"At the moment I don't even think I know what love is," she replied with bitter amusement, resting her tense neck against the back of the seat. "I'm learning what it isn't. We've been so close all our lives, Clay. It seemed so natural and right that we get married. Now, I'm beginning to wonder if we both reached that conclusion for the wrong reason."

"I care about you more than any woman I've ever met. I love you, Cathie," Clay declared earnestly.

"I feel the same." Pain tightened its hold around her throat. "We both need time to think this over. We're too confused to be sure of our own emotions and what we really feel."

He eagerly seized on her implied suggestion to postpone the discussion. He needed time to think coherently over these sudden doubts. "It's late," he agreed, not seeing the cynical smile that turned up the corners of Cathie's mouth. "Things will look different after a night's sleep. All this talk will turn out to be premarital nerves, a lot of smoke without any fire."

"I hope you're right," she said, opening her car door and climbing out. "Don't bother to see me to the door, Clay. Let's just call it a night."

Cathie was in the house with the door closed and locked behind her before she heard the car motor start. She glanced down at the ring on her finger and knew she wouldn't be wearing it much longer.

CHAPTER TEN

CATHIE'S PREMONITION had proved correct. Her finger was bare. Clay's attempts on the evening following the Fourth to dissuade her from returning it had been halfhearted and lacking conviction.

The termination of her engagement was a mixed blessing. Now Cathie was free, but free to do what? To fall in love with Rob Douglas? When she had been engaged, her thoughts had never been far from him. Now, they were always centered on him. Besides, Rob had made it clear the night at the lake that he didn't enter into her life at all. She had been a method of amusement for him, a mild flirtation.

Over a week had passed, a week of staring into space while the minutes dragged by, a week of being the object of understanding looks from the people she knew. They thought her melancholy abstraction was caused by her broken engagement. They couldn't know that Cathie was seeking ways to bump casually into Rob and inform him of the current change. That desire was mixed with dread. Rob had been the one to point out the error of her emotions. Would he applaud her break with Clay or mock her inability to make the discovery on her own?

Her heavy sigh broke the stillness of the room

as she turned her gaze away from the window and the golden twilight signaling the approach of night. The coo of a mourning dove matched the sad, silent sounds of her own heart. Andy glanced sympathetically in Cathie's direction before returning her attention to the book on her lap.

Clay had wanted to keep on seeing Cathie, but she had been adamant in her refusal. There was the fear that because Rob didn't care, she and Clay would drift back together in their old pattern and they would both suffer from it. But right now, Cathie would have been glad of his company. Anything to relieve these tortuous moments of wanting to see Rob and not having the courage to carry out her desire.

The shrill ring of the telephone was a welcome interruption and Cathie sprang to her feet to answer it. Perhaps it was Clay. If it was, she would invite him over for coffee and they would talk over old times and alleviate this tormenting thought of Rob. With that occupying her mind, it was a shock to hear Mrs. Carver's voice on the other end of the line.

"Is that you, Cathie?" Rob's housekeeper demanded.

"Yes. What's wrong?" she breathed quickly.

"My daughter Sharon just called me. They've rushed my grandson to the hospital with an appendicitis attack," she explained with a rush. "She wants me to come just as soon as I can."

For one terrifying minute Cathie had thought something had happened to Rob before she soberly realized that Mrs. Carver wouldn't have thought to notify her if there had. "Do you need a ride? I'm not busy. I can be out there in a few minutes."

"No, I have a car. I called because Mr. Douglas had to drive to Omaha and won't be back until late this evening. And I can't go off and leave Tad here alone. As late as it is, I can't take him to the hospital with me because heaven knows what time I'll be back. I didn't know of anyone else other than you I could call on the spur of the moment to stay with Tad. The two of you are quite good friends and he trusts you."

Cathie paused. "You want me to stay with Tad?"

"Until Mr. Douglas comes back or I come back from the hospital. Would you, Cathie? I'd feel so much easier knowing you were with Tad. I'm sure Mr. Douglas wouldn't object."

"Of course, I'll come," Cathie agreed, her spirits lifting at the prospect of possibly seeing Rob. Besides, the need for her to go to the farm was genuine. There was nothing engineered about it. And Cathie knew she was the likely choice to watch Tad. She was in full agreement with Mrs. Carver that he shouldn't be left alone or carted off to the hospital.

"Thank you." The housekeeper's gratitude flooded over the line. "I'll ring Sharon at the hospital and let her know I'll be leaving as soon as you get here."

"I'll leave immediately," Cathie assured her before exchanging goodbyes.

As Cathie walked into the door of the farm-house, Mrs. Carver walked out. Tad was quite delighted at the change, finding Cathie a willing listener to the tales of his escapades with Charlie Smith, who was now both playmate and bosom friend. Patience, Tad's half-grown yellow kitten, had become a house guest and Cathie was duly introduced to him.

Although she tucked Tad into his bed at the top of the stairs at ten o'clock, it was a half hour later before he actually fell asleep. The last program on television didn't interest her. Cathie's thoughts were too preoccupied with Rob's eventual return to become interested in the simple plottings of an old movie. At last she flicked the set off, her gaze shifting to the closed parlor doors. She couldn't help wondering how much further Rob had got in his remodeling of the room into a den.

Opening the heavy walnut double doors, Cathie gasped at the complete transformation of the room. The satiny sheen of the walnut paneling and shelves gave the room a rich glow, echoed by the vibrant gold carpeting. The two overstuffed chairs that had been previously hidden by protective sheets were covered in a rich gold and brown plaid that fitted so well in the masculine room. Books lined the shelves and as her fingers trailed over the titles, Cathie saw they ranged from reference books to reading material.

Her glowing eyes roamed admiringly over the room. There was no remorse over the loss of the parlor; the room that had been used only once a year at Christmas time. This was a room a person would want to be in all year through, a cozy snug room that beckoned one to come and sit. As she lifted a mystery book from the shelves bearing the author's name of Robert Douglas, Cathie longed to do just that, but she decided to forgo that pleasure in favor of the sun porch where she could view Rob's eventual arrival.

The night was sultry with heat lightning dancing across the southern skies. Although the walls of the old farmhouse were thick to keep the house cool in the heat of the summer and warm in the cold of the winter, the sighing south-east breeze that filtered through the open windows of the sun porch was a refreshing addition. Cathie propped herself on the blue-flowered chaise longue, flicking on the switch of the overhead reading lamp.

With each page she turned, she became more and more engrossed in the suspense-filled mystery. The fluttering of a moth outside the window as it beat its wings futilely against the screen was unnoticed. The rasping screech of the crickets' song was ignored along with the drone of the cicadas. Not even the eerie hooting call of a hunting owl drew her attention away from the printed pages.

It was two in the morning when Cathie finished reading the book, the closed pages remaining in her lap. Stifling a yawn, she glanced at her watch, surprised by how quickly the time had passed and understanding why she had such difficulty focusing her eyes on the last pages. She gazed out the window at the galaxy of stars sprinkled over the blue-velvet sky and wondered how much longer it would be before Rob came home.

The merry songs of sparrows, robins, flickers and thrushes all blended together, their melodic sounds broken by the crowing of a rooster. Cathie's eyes opened slowly to focus on the golden kiss of dawn. Morning—it couldn't be! Cathie blinked the last of the sleep from her eyes. Her blond head turned swiftly away from the windows as she realized that Rob hadn't come back.

A momentary shaft of fear struck her until she saw the man sleeping in the chair, his feet stretched out on an ottoman and his head propped against his arm in an uncomfortable position. A blue sports jacket lay over the back of the matching wicker chair while his tie remained loosely knotted around his neck and the white shirt unbuttoned revealing the smooth column of his throat. Rob looked so peaceful, his hair attractively disheveled as if he had raked his fingers through it before falling into an exhausted sleep. Cathie had no idea what time Rob had got back. Not a sound had disturbed her sleep, yet the light above her head had been turned off.

Very quietly she rose to her feet, setting the book that had been on her lap on a nearby table, and tiptoed into the kitchen. The wall clock showed it was a few minutes before six o'clock. Making as little noise as possible, Cathie put the coffee on before making her way to the bathroom. After sleeping in her blue slacks and the yellow and blue striped top, she knew she was a rumpled mess. She washed the remnants of the sandman's visit from her face and applied the lipstick and mascara from her purse to her mouth and lashes before running a comb through her tousled short curls. Already the wrinkles were beginning to disappear from the synthetic material of her clothes.

Pleased by her reflection in the mirror, Cathie walked back into the kitchen, her steps as light-hearted as her spirits. There was supreme contentment in knowing Rob was in the next room. The electric percolator was just emitting its last sighing pop when she walked in. She sniffed appreciatively at the fragrant steam as she filled a mug from the cupboard.

"Would you pour me a cup of that coffee, too?"

A wild leaping of her heart followed Rob's words as she spun around to stare at the tall, imposing figure framed in the kitchen doorway. "I . . . I didn't mean to wake you," Cathie stumbled before recovering her poise.

"You didn't." He smiled, walking farther into the room. "It was the aroma of that coffee. It sends out its own wake-up signals."

She reached in the cupboard for another over-sized mug and filled it with coffee, then carried both to the dinette table where Rob was now sitting. "I didn't hear you come in last night."

"I know." His brown eyes moved lazily over her face with that velvet quality that was soothing yet so disturbing. "What happened to Mrs. Carver?"

"Her grandson was rushed to the hospital last night with an appendicitis attack, and she asked me to stay with Tad," Cathie explained, choosing a chair opposite Rob.

She was hesitant to meet his eyes squarely, afraid that her inner excitement would be revealed. No other man had ever been able to make her senses so conscious of his presence the way Rob did. This was love and not fleeting physical attraction. And there was the realization, as she sat across the table from him with the dawn just breaking outside, that she had always loved him, almost from the first day she had met him. A fine line divided love and hate, two equally explosive emotions. Cathie had looked on Rob as an enemy, a usurper, but with a secret smile she knew it was because he was stealing her heart and not the Homeplace. Still, it was impossible to admit any of this to Rob.

Her gaze moved unconsciously from the dark liquid in her cup to the equally dark but shadowed and enigmatic expression in Rob's eyes. It was then that she realized a silence had descended on them. The unreadable look in his eyes made her uneasy.

"It must have been quite late when you got back," she said, wrapping her trembling fingers around the cup. "I know it was after two when I dozed off. You should have wakened me when you came in." Although she was unutterably glad he hadn't.

Rob sipped his coffee, lowering his gaze from her face. "It was nearly four in the morning. It didn't make any sense to wake you from a sound sleep to send you home to try to go back to sleep."

There was such a natural vitality and alertness about him that Cathie found it hard to believe that he had only had two hours' sleep himself. Yet he looked refreshed and rested. She wanted to suggest that he catch a few more hours of sleep, but she didn't know of any way to word it without sounding over-solicitous.

"I don't need any more sleep." A crooked smile touched his mouth as he perceptively read her thoughts. "But I could eat some bacon and eggs. How about you?"

With a self-conscious laugh, Cathie agreed, assuring him that she wasn't a novice in the kitchen. Once she had the bacon sizzling in the pan, she began setting the table while Rob excused himself to wash up.

"You didn't mention how you liked the book," Rob commented, walking back into the room with his hair combed and in place and bringing the clean scent of soap.

"Oh, I enjoyed it," she said fervently, then laughed. "That sounds off hand, doesn't it?" she asked, tossing him a smiling glance over her shoulder. "I just realized how hard it is to sound sincere when you're talking to the person who actually wrote the book you just read. But it's true. I honestly couldn't put it down until I'd read the last page."

"That's sufficent praise for anyone." He stood near the stove watching as Cathie broke two eggs and slid them into the hot melted lard in the pan. "I like my eggs over easy with toast and jam on the side."

Over their breakfast meal, Rob explained that he had driven to Omaha to meet a representative from his publishing firm who had stopped over en route to Los Angeles. Cathie received the impression that this representative was also a personal friend, but Rob didn't reveal if it was a male or female. She shifted the conversation to his past life, lightheartedly matching reminiscences of their childhood growing up on a farm.

"How did you get that scar near your eye?" Cathie asked when Rob mentioned his tour of duty in the armed forces.

"The truth?" His eyes gleamed with wicked mischief. He touched the scar lightly as he grinned. "I received this when I fell off my bicycle at the age of six. Not a very adventurous story, is it?"

Cathie laughingly agreed, and began the task of clearing the table. It was a pleasant surprise when Rob joined her. With the two of them, it took almost no time at all to wash up.

"What time does Tad get up?" Cathie asked as she put away the dish cloth and hung up the dish towel Rob had been using.

"Around eight. Luckily he's not like me. A bowl of cereal and some juice can carry him until lunchtime," Rob said, shrugging and pouring them each a cup of coffee and carrying it onto the sun porch. After they were both comfortably seated in wicker chairs, he turned his gaze toward her with bland watchfulness. "What have you been doing with yourself lately?"

Cathie took a deep breath. This was her chance to tell him she had broken her engagement to Clay. "Not really very much. I'm getting kind of anxious for school to start again so I can have something to do." There was a pause while she stared at the shimmering liquid in her cup as it caught the sunlight that streamed through the window. "Clay and I broke up."

"I know you did," he said, meeting her startled look easily. "You forget this is a small town. The local grapevine passed that message around the day after you gave him his ring back."

A very small "oh" came from her lips.

"What now? Are you trying to find someone else to fill the empty niche in your fantasy?" There was a sharp, biting note in his voice.

"What do you mean?" Cathie asked in a tight voice made weak by the constriction in her throat.

"You don't have Clay around any more. Surely you must be looking for another partner to act out your childhood dream. I imagine as the new owner of the Homeplace I would be a likely candidate." His gaze was penetrating and harsh. Cathie couldn't meet it squarely.

The Homeplace. How strange! A few months ago it was all so important to her. Every room held some precious memory, and yet last night the only thing she had been conscious of was how much of Rob's presence was in every room. From the outside, it still looked like the farm home of her grandparents, but on the inside where the living was done, the house was unmistakably Rob's. No, Cathie could honestly say to herself that Rob's ownership of the Homeplace had nothing to do with her love for him. One look at the grim expression on his face told her that he didn't believe her.

"You would be a perfect choice," she agreed, pride making her lift her chin, forcing her to ignore the tears rising to intensify the green of her eyes. "Except that I've made a pact with myself that I'll only marry the man I truly love."

One eyebrow flickered into an arch before settling back to match the other. "Do you mean you've given up your dream so easily?" The disbelief in his voice mocked her.

"It wasn't easy." Gratefully she let her gaze slide from his to glance around the room and outside to the cornfields at the edge of the lawn and garden. "I'll miss this place. Some of my happiest moments were here." *Including those with you,* she added silently. "But I think I have my priorities in the right order now, and it doesn't include a marriage of convenience anymore."

"That's good." Cathie felt his gaze narrowing on her as she continued to look away. An indignant anger and hurt pride were making themselves felt, generated by the pain in her heart. "You wouldn't have found me to be an amenable suitor like Clay."

"I don't consider you a suitor at all!" The lie to save face leaped easily out as Cathie rose to her feet. "I really think it's time I left. I'm sure you're capable of looking after your own son when he gets up."

Rob was on his feet, towering over her until she was robbed of her breath. His gaze was so penetrating that she felt sure he must guess the truth of her feelings.

"I appreciate you coming out here last night on such short notice," was all he said.

"I did it for Tad," Cathie declared vigorously.

"I never have thanked you for the time you spent with him."

"Don't bother." The tears were so close to spilling over her lashes that Cathie grabbed her purse and bolted for the door.

It was heartbreaking to discover there was no way mere words could ever convince Rob that she could care for him as a person and not as the owner of the Homeplace. Even if she could, he gave no indication he was interested in accepting the heart she would give him so willingly. No, she was only of use to him because of Tad. And now that Tad had adjusted to his new life, Rob didn't care about her anymore.

CHAPTER ELEVEN

"YOU'VE BEEN UNNATURALLY QUIET, Cathie."
Andy glanced curiously at the girl walking
beside her. "All through lunch you didn't say
two words except to nod your head yes or no to
whatever I said."

"Is that so unusual?" The brittle smile
couldn't reach the dull green eyes. Cathie
sighed, turning her gaze away from her roommate's probing eyes to study the rolling, dark
gray clouds slowly billowing over the entire sky
and the incredibly still trees with not a breath of
wind stirring their leaves. "I don't know, maybe
it's the weather." Or Rob Douglas, her mind
added, sending a twisting dagger of pain to her
heart.

"Well, the forecast predicts thunder showers."
Andy's brown eyes turned skyward, too, as she
plucked at her nylon uniform clinging stickily to
her skin. "And those clouds look as if they're
going to burst any minute. It will probably be
raining when I get off work tonight, since I left
my umbrella at home."

When they neared the corner where they
would separate, Cathie to go home and Andy to
return to the dental office, the first fat raindrops
splattered on the dust-covered pavement.
Andy's palm turned upward to assure herself it
was raining.

"It isn't going to wait until this afternoon," she declared, looking at the droplet on her hand. "I'm going to make a dash for the office before I get drenched." She was already moving away from Cathie at a brisk pace. "I'll see you tonight."

Cathie returned the wave, making her steps swifter as she crossed to the other side of the street. The rain was falling faster now as the air around her became more muggy but with a fragrant cleanness. For several blocks, the rainfall was steady and gentle, like a tepid shower. Cathie couldn't bring her feet to hurry despite the growing dampness of her peasant top and the gold-colored slacks. There was no desire to return to the emptiness of the house that she had done her best to avoid these past four days. She wanted no time to think about Rob Douglas, or the torment of her situation would be more difficult to bear.

Thunder rumbled as darker clouds rolled overhead, accompanied by darting tongues of lightning. The air became slightly cooler, stirring up a sighing breeze that gradually grew into a wind. As Cathie made her turn half a block from her house, the drops began falling closer together, driven now by the wind. Common sense made her sprint the short distance to the door rather than risk a complete soaking. At the closing of the door behind her, a fiery flash of lightning split open the clouds and sent torrents of water to ricochet off the ground.

The gusting wind was whipping the rain through the open windows. Cathie scrambled hastily to close them before the water could do more than dampen the floors and furniture. After she had wiped the small pools under the windows, she turned the towel on herself, blotting away the few drops that were still clinging to her skin. There were few gaps between the roaring thunder and the streaking lightning. She felt a kinship with the violent storm as if its fury was unleashing her own pent-up emotions and bringing some measure of relief.

Curling up on the sofa with her arms wrapped around her knees, Cathie stared out the window at the angled sheets of driving rain. It hammered at the quaking leaves of bushes and trees and beat down the drowning blades of grass. The birds, squirrels, rabbits, and all the rest of the little creatures had taken shelter from the deluge. Cathie's head came up with a start. Duchess! There was no covering flap on her kennel and the rain would be beating in unmercifully. Cathie raced toward the door, pausing only to take the clear plastic, bubble-shaped umbrella from the closet. Paying no heed to the buffeting rain, she headed straight for the kennel, scolding herself for forgetting the aging shepherd.

"Duchess! Come on, girl," she called coaxingly before dropping to one knee beside the small dark opening. No red gold nose came out. The sky had darkened ominously, making it difficult to see in the dim interior, but a searching hand ascertained that Duchess wasn't inside. The metallic gleam of the chain half hidden by grass caught her eye, and lifting it, Cathie saw the rusty broken link and knew that Duchess had run away.

There was no telling how long she had been gone since Cathie couldn't remember seeing the dog when she had dashed in the house a quarter of an hour earlier. And she had been gone all morning, which gave the shepherd ample time to break free and run off.

As the rain began darkening her unprotected gold slacks, Cathie debated whether or not to go in search of the dog. Its final destination, she knew, would be the farm. The question was, had Duchess already reached it or was she en route? Cathie tried to convince herself that the dog would take shelter, but visions of soft, trusting eyes and the graying muzzle wouldn't go away. It was foolish to try to find Duchess in a storm that showed no signs of letting up. Cathie argued with herself all the way to her car.

The windshield wipers had little effect on the onslaught of rain as the car crept along the highway with Cathie peering out of the rain-streaked windows for a glimpse of the dog. At every place that offered any sort of protection for the shepherd, she rolled the window down, ignoring the biting spray on her face to search for the telltale red gold color. The big tree loomed ahead of her at the intersection of the county road and the highway. The Homeplace was only a quarter of a mile west on that graveled road.

Cathie inhaled deeply. "Well," she sighed aloud, "I've come this far, so I might as well go all the way."

Her car tires slushed onto the sodden gravel road. The air rumbled with repeated rolls of thunder that seemed to match the quaking going on in her own body. She parked the car near the machine shed, wishing there was a place where it would be out of sight. Snatching the umbrella from the passenger seat, she scrambled out of the car to dash toward the corn crib. The soaking wind tore her pleading calls for Duchess from her throat, drowning them in the fury of the storm. Faintly she heard an answering yelp. There, framed in the machine shed doors, sat Duchess.

Cathie dashed into the rain, her sandals slipping and sliding in the mud. The remnants of the leash was still attached to the shepherd's collar. Cathie had but one thought—to get the dog from the machine shed to the car. But Duchess had an entirely different idea as she retreated farther away from her mistress into the dark recesses of the shed. With a diving grab, Cathie caught hold of the leash and began the thankless task of dragging the reluctant dog to the doorway.

The umbrella had to be abandoned since Cathie couldn't manage the dog and the umbrella at the same time. She paused in the doorway to catch her breath and assess the distance from the shed to the car. Through rain-spiked lashes, she studied the path that was quickly becoming a quagmire and wondered how much of a fuss Duchess would put up between here and there. If only the dog were human, she could explain why she didn't want to stay in the shelter of the machine shed. Why it was so important to leave before Rob discovered she had been here.

A blinding flash of electrically charged fire raced jaggedly across the sky, momentarily darkening the pupils of her green eyes. Her gaze scanned the clouds. With a sharp intake of breath, she saw the dark finger snake out of a cloud, its weaving funnel dancing above the ground before disappearing back into the clouds. She had lived in Iowa too long not to recognize a tornado, however far away it might be. Duchess whined and pulled backward on the leash, and instantly Cathie fell to her knees and threw her arms around the dog's neck.

"What are we going to do? We can't leave now!" Closing her eyes tightly against the panic that leaped in her chest, she buried her head for a moment in the damp hair of the shepherd's neck.

"I thought I was seeing things when I spotted your car parked down here!" an angry voice barked above her head.

Cathie remembered to keep a hold on the leash as she jumped to her feet, her wide frightened eyes turning on Rob while her heart hammered away somewhere in the area of her throat.

"Don't just stand there!" He reached out to grasp her wrist. "Didn't you see that funnel cloud? We have to get under cover."

"Duchess," Cathie murmured protestingly, foolishly thinking of the shepherd instead of herself. "I can't go without her."

Rob cursed silently under his breath as he picked up the whimpering dog and ordered Cathie to go ahead of him. "Go to the root cellar behind the house!" he shouted.

Without the shelter of a roof, she was drenched by the pounding rain in seconds. Widened green eyes kept scanning the clouds, knowing that at any second another funnel might be born. Blocking out the sound of thunderous claps and explosive fireballs, she tried to keep her ears tuned for that terrifying sound of a hundred jet engines. Cathie was gasping for breath when she reached the slanted wooden door that led down to the root cellar. Rob was at her heels, the sodden dog limp and quivering in his arms. It took all her fear-weakened strength to lift the door for Rob to precede her. The small electric bulb shining at the bottom of the steps was a beacon light leading to security and safety. Cathie tumbled down the stairs toward it, letting the door slam shut overhead.

The scent of potatoes, apples and pears all mingled with the odor of the musty earthen walls. Duchess didn't bother to shake the water from her saturated coat but scrambled beneath the jar-laden shelves the instant Rob set her on her feet. Now that the race to safety was over Cathie's legs were no longer capable of holding her up. She forced them to carry her to an upright crate where she collapsed with quivering relief.

"Where's Tad?" The thought of the boy somewhere out there in the storm struck fear in her heart.

"Over at the Smiths'," Rob answered calmly in spite of the angry frown creasing his stern features. "I called over a half hour ago when I heard the tornado warning on the radio. They're all safe in their basement. And Mrs. Carver is at the hospital with her grandson. What were you doing out in this?"

Cathie wiped the excess water from her forehead that kept trickling down from her hair. "Duchess ran away and I couldn't face the thought of her being out in the storm. I knew she'd come here."

"Of all the stupid . . . ." His mouth clamped tightly shut on the rest of his words. "Didn't you even have the radio on in your car?"

He was standing above her, the pale green print shirt plastered to his wide shoulders accenting every rippling muscle. At the brief negative movement of her head, he sighed in exasperation and raked his fingers through his curling hair.

"How long do you think this will last?" Cathie asked, involuntarily flinching as a resounding crash of lightning made itself heard through the thick earthen walls that muffled all but the loudest sounds.

"Half an hour, an hour." Rob shrugged dismissively as if time was of little consequence. "It depends on how large a cell this storm is."

As he walked toward the stairwell, Cathie noticed the portable radio and flashlight sitting on the shelf near the exit. Rob flicked the radio on to a local station, and the serene melody of a popular ballad filled the air.

Impatiently his gaze slid over her. "I didn't think to bring a towel or blanket to dry ourselves with."

A burning rush of color flamed in her face,

and she knew that her own cotton top was just
as revealing in its wetness as his had been. "I
don't mind," she murmured.

Water dripped from the ventilation shaft,
sounding much louder than the steady hammer
of rain on the wooden door. The shepherd was
still cowering under the shelves, her ears flat
against her head and her eyes, wide and frightened by the violence outside. Cathie silently
wished that Rob would stop pacing back and
forth like a caged panther. The small muggy cellar was becoming charged with an unbearable
tension, and she knew her racing pulse no longer
had anything to do with the storm taking place
outside. Trivial conversation was impossible for
Cathie. She was too conscious of Rob as the
man she loved and not as a fellow human being
trapped by the storm.

The explosive report of striking lightning
threw the dimly lit cellar into complete darkness. Cathie leaped to her feet. The shriek torn
from her throat was generated more from surprise than genuine fear. Before she could
recover her wits, Rob's arms were around her,
drawing her against the firmness of his body.

"The power went out, that's all," he murmured, holding her in the protective circle.

For a moment Cathie couldn't move or
breathe, so overwhelming was the desire to slip
her arms around him and lift her head from his
muscular chest for his kiss. His previous rejec-
tion of her made the natural impulse impossible
to carry out, another humiliation more than her
pride could bear. Unwillingly she held herself

away, his arms not letting her escape altogether, but she was free from the hypnotic beat of his heart beneath her head. A quivering sigh raced over her body.

"You're cold," Rob observed, his voice coming from somewhere near the top of her head.

"So are you," she answered quickly, her fingers still touching the cool dampness of his shirt that clung to his firm waistline like a second skin. "It's . . . it's these wet clothes."

"As soon as this storm eases, we can change into something dry."

Cathie was grateful for the darkness that concealed the torment his nearness was causing. "Yes," she agreed, attempting to shift out of his arms.

But he tightened his hold. "It would be best if you stayed close to me to ward off the chance of a chill."

"No, no, I'm all right," she protested, pushing ineffectually against his chest.

"Don't turn female on me, Cat," he said angrily, pulling her roughly against him. "I'm not going to try to seduce you."

She had not the strength or will to fight him as he maneuvered through the darkness to the crate, easing her down to the earthen floor so the two of them could use if for a backrest. Weakly Cathie let him cradle her in his arms, the burning warmth of his body sapping what little opposition remained. For an eternity of minutes they remained there, with Rob never commenting on the rigidity of Cathie's slender frame.

Rob moved slightly, lifting his arm from around her shoulders. "The rain seems to have let up. I'm going to check to see what it looks like out there." He reached above their heads for the flashlight, mercifully not shining it on Cathie's pale, strained face.

The beam of light picked out the path to the wooden steps. As the hinges creaked on the overhead door, the disc jockey on the radio station said that the worst of the storm seemed to have passed. With the cellar door opened, partially illuminating the underground room, Cathie could tell the falling rain had a more gentle patter to it. At the sound of Rob's shoes descending the stairs, she rose to her feet inhaling deeply and attempting to wipe the nervous strain from her face.

"Its safe to go inside now," said Rob, his face shadowed by the gray light coming over his shoulder from the opened door.

As if in confirmation of his words, the cellar light came back on, only to be switched off by Rob as Cathie walked past him to the steps. Duchess was much more reluctant to leave their shelter, consenting only after several repeated commands. Then the shepherd raced around the house, heading for the comparative safety beneath the front porch. Rob's swinging stride brought him abreast of Cathie as they walked swiftly toward the back door. Stealing a glance from the corner of her eye, she watched him run an appraising look over the farm seeking signs of the storm's damage to his property. None was visible except for a few broken tree limbs.

Cathie couldn't help wondering if the Smith farm and Tad had fared as well.

Once they entered the house Rob made straight for the telephone, and Cathie knew his thoughts were on his son. She waited anxiously while he put the call through. After a brief exchange of words, the grim lines around his mouth eased into a smile which he cast over his shoulder to Cathie, signifying that Tad was all right. She smiled tremulously back, her heart singing that Rob should be so perceptive of her thoughts.

"No damage at the Smiths' either, and Tad is fine," Rob said, turning to her after he had replaced the receiver. "I talked to Ray. From what he's been able to find out from his neighbors, the few tornadoes that were sighted all stayed in the air, although the accompanying winds did take a few trees."

"That's a blessing," Cathie agreed, blinking at the acid burning of tears in her eyes for caring so much about what happened to Rob's son. But the subsequent shuddering of her shoulders was from relief at knowing Tad was safe and unharmed.

"There's a robe hanging on the bathroom door," Rob said, misinterpreting her shiver. "After you get out of those wet clothes, you'd better take a hot bath."

"What about you?"

"I'll use the shower downstairs." Cathie started to turn away, feeling foolish for voicing her concern for his well-being. "Set your clothes outside the bathroom door," Rob added, "and

I'll toss them in the clothes dryer in the basement. It shouldn't take more than a few minutes to get them dry."

Cathie hadn't realized how chilled she was until she slipped out of her wet clothes, wrapped herself in the large terrycloth robe and set the clothes outside the bathroom door while the tub was filling with water. She knew she should have insisted on leaving immediately rather than prolong her stay with Rob, but it had been so much easier giving in to the authority in his tone. As she crawled into the tubful of hot water, she was glad she had stayed. The water was a balm to her raw nerves as it eased the aching tension of her muscles held so tightly in check when she had rested against Rob. She lay in the tub gaining strength from the soothing caress of the water until she heard Rob moving around in the kitchen.

There was a rap on the door. "I've poured you a cup of coffee," Rob called out from the other side.

"I'll be out in a minute," she answered, stirring herself into mobility even though she could have used a longer respite from his presence.

Rob barely glanced up when she padded into the room minutes later, the robe securely belted around her waist. "Sit down." He motioned toward the table, sliding a glance in her direction over his shoulder.

Her green eyes were drawn admiringly to his crisp appearance in his fawn-colored trousers and a complementing silk shirt. When he turned away from the counter carrying her cup of coffee, she veiled her look with dark lashes. He stopped beside her chair, brushing her arm as he set the cup down and causing a renewed fluttering in her stomach. Involuntarily she drew away.

"Your clothes will be dry in a few more minutes," Rob said abruptly, moving away to lean against the kitchen counter.

There was a burning intensity to his brown eyes as he studied her lowered head. Cathie took the cup of coffee in her hand, seeking to divert her attention from his magnetic attraction. She took a healthy-sized swallow of the medium-hot liquid. Instantly her throat burned and she began coughing and sputtering, not from the heat of the coffee but because of the liberal lacing of whisky it contained.

"Why didn't you tell me?" she demanded hoarsely. Her eyes were watering from the potency of the liquor. The choking sensation remained as she rose from her chair and walked to the sink to pour the remainder of the liquid in the cup down the drain.

"Because I presumed you would do exactly what you just did," he answered sharply. "This way you drank at least some of it down." His dark eyes raked her form, still shuddering from the aftereffects of the drink. "As shaky as you were out there in the cellar, trembling like a half-drowned kitten, I thought you needed it."

"Storms like that don't terrify me. I grew up with them." Her knuckles were white from the way she was gripping the cup so tightly. "You were imagining things."

"Then why were you quivering like jelly in my arms?" Rob demanded with a derisive laugh.

Now it was her chin that was trembling as Cathie tried to salvage a bit of her pride and self-respect. "Maybe I just couldn't stand to have you touch me," she spat out sarcastically, needing to deny the havoc his touch caused in her.

The angry fire in his gaze seared over her as his arms shot out to imprison her shoulders. "Damn, but I'm tired of you always lashing out at me as if I was a whipping boy supposed to take your insults without any protest!"

He drew her roughly against the rock hardness of his chest. Her arms were pinned against him by her own body and the iron bank of his arms held her there. Twining his fingers in the golden curls of her hair, Rob forced her head up, staring into the jade eyes sparkling with diamond tears.

"Please, please let me go," she whispered. The hard contours of his body were destroying all her weakly constructed defenses, the desire to surrender almost impossible to withstand.

The soft, persuasive velvet look was gone from his eyes, replaced by ebony-hard coals that glowed with avenging anger. "You're an independent feline creature, aren't you?" Rob mocked. "Coolly aloof and sarcastic when it suits you, other times hissing and showing your claws." His gaze narrowed on her lips, moistly parted and tremulous. "It's time I heard you really purr."

"N-no!" Cathie breathed, already being

brought closer to the sensual line of his mouth. But there was only the barest glimmer of a smile on his lips before they took hers captive.

There was no place to withdraw to, away from the feverish heat building under the consummate kiss. Her head was pressed back against his shoulder, the short honey-colored curls clinging to the silk shirt while the sweet savageness of his mouth received the response it demanded. Here was a storm as tempestuous as anything the heavens could create. Golden lightning bolts touched off more burning fires inside while thunder roared in her ears, and Cathie was swept away by the whirling winds of his embrace.

Her arms that had been crushed between their bodies found their way around his neck, bringing her still closer to him. The caressing movements of his hands on her back molded her tighter, the combustion of her surrender changing his lips from demanding to possessive. Rob's breathing, too, was ragged as he explored the sensitive cord in her neck and the tan hollow of her shoulder.

"Rob," she murmured, aching for the feel of his lips against hers again and moving her head until she found them. It was agony when he dragged his mouth away again.

"Damn you," Rob muttered into her hair as he crushed her tightly against him. His breath fanned her ears before he moved his head away to stare into her questioning and hurt viridescent eyes. "I swore I wouldn't let you bewitch me. First Yvette used me to escape the dream world of her parents and now you want me to fulfill your own dream world. There's poetic justice in that!"

"Rob . . . ." The words formed on her lips to dispel his assumption.

"Don't you see it doesn't matter!" he said, tossing back his head to laugh bitterly before bringing his scornful gaze back to her pleading face. "I've fallen in love with you," he declared grimly, unmindful of the exultant disbelief sparkling now in her eyes. "I don't care why you want me. All I want to know is that you're mine!" An eyebrow arched at the look of dismay. "Where's the triumphant smile, Cat? Surely the taste of victory is sweet? I knew you were lying that morning when you said you weren't considering me to take Clay's place. I could see it in your face."

"Rob, you don't understand. I don't want you to take Clay's place. I never loved Clay," Cathie began earnestly, "not like I love you." Her fingers covered the cynical curl of his mouth. "It has nothing to do with the Homeplace, the farm. It never did, except at the beginning when I hated you for buying it." She swallowed nervously at the still doubting look on his face. "How can I make you understand that I'm telling you the truth? You can sell the Homeplace, burn it to the ground, do whatever you want, and I'll still love you. You can take me to New York or the Arctic Circle. All I want is to be with you." Her hands moved lovingly over his face, savoring each feature of the handsome lines. "All I want is to be yours."

His fingers bit into her shoulders as his dark eyes examined her face. "It's true," she breathed again, letting all the love she had tried to conceal shine in her eyes. "I do love you."

"Then why ...." His eyes raced over her face. "Why did you put me through this hell?"

"I was going through it myself. The hardest thing to realize was that I loved you. When I finally admitted it to myself you made it clear that you expected me to pursue you in order to get the farm." A small smile curved her mouth. "A girl has some pride, you know, and until this moment I didn't believe that you actually cared for me."

"Oh, Cat!" he laughed exultantly. "I do!" He swung her completely off the floor to rain kisses on her face, before finally settling on her mouth in one long, breathtaking kiss. They were both stunned by the passion-charged minutes when Rob lifted his head some time later. "I think you'd better go and get your clothes out of the dryer and put them on damp or dry, or I'm not going to be responsible for my actions," he murmured huskily.

With a tinkling laugh of pleasure, Cathie slipped out of his arms, the feverish color of her face revealing that she was truly his to command. There was a sharp intake of breath from Rob at the love radiating so openly from her green eyes, eyes that she knew would never tire of looking at him.

"Go," he ordered gruffly, and she dutifully glided toward the stairwell to the basement. As her bare foot touched the first step, his voice halted her. She turned to drink in the sight of the lean frame a few steps away. "Did you mean it, Cat, when you said you would go back to New York with me?"

"Yes," she replied without any hesitation.

"What about the farm?"

She smiled widely, understanding his need to be reassured of the genuineness of her love. "I'll miss it because basically I'm a country girl. But my homeplace is where ever you are, Rob. It's the most important thing in the world to me for you to believe that."

"I do," he said nodding, a possessively tender light shining from his eyes.

Cathie wanted to cross the space that separated them and feel again the heady excitement of being in his arms. But considering the present state of their emotions that was too dangerous. Instead she turned and floated down the stairs, changing into her dry clothes in record time. Rob was standing in front of the windows in the sun porch, a cup of coffee in his hand, and staring out the window when she ascended the last flight.

"Look," he said, darting an admiring glance in her direction before motioning with his head out the window. She walked swiftly to his side and was immediately nestled against his shoulder as she looked out the window. A multicolored rainbow was arching out of the dissipating clouds, shimmering with jewel-like colors of sapphire, emerald, amethyst, topaz and carnelian. The entire countryside was etched in sharp relief, the air washed clean of all dust particles to vividly reveal the rolling fields of corn, wheat and hay, dotted by trees and buildings.

Cathie sighed. "It will be hard to leave all this beauty."

"Who said we were?" Rob's gaze turned tenderly to her bemused face.

"You did." Her eyes widened with blinking bewilderment.

"No," he smiled. "You brought it up, and I only verified that if I asked you to leave the farm for New York that you would. I have no intention of ever leaving here."

"That's too wonderful to be true!" Cathie gasped, covering a little sob of happiness. "I feel I should give up something I cherish to prove that I love you and not what you own."

"I have a better idea. Why don't you spend the rest of your life proving that you love me? That would truly be heaven on earth."

His head was moving to take her up on the invitation written on her parted lips when the back door slammed. They turned in unison as Tad raced up the steps. He showed not the slightest surprise to see Cathie as he greeted them together.

"Hi, dad. Hi, Cathie. Mr. Smith brought me home so you wouldn't be worried about me. Boy, that was some storm!" His words were tumbling over each other in his excitement. "Charlie and me saw a tornado! But it never came down out of the sky."

"We saw it, too," Rob said, nodding and holding Cathie tighter when she would have moved away. "I'm glad you're home, son. I wanted to ask you what you thought about Cathie and me getting married." A teasing light danced over her flushed cheeks. "I have to get my proposal in to make it official."

"Really?" Tad's hazel eyes grew enormously large. "That would be terrific!" Then he stopped, a smile running from cheek to cheek. "Especially since you won't be my teacher next year."

"We'll go see your parents this weekend," said Rob, gazing into her tremulous expression. "That is, if you are going to marry me."

"Yes," Cathie breathed.

"I forgot to tell you," Tad inserted. "When we drove past the pasture, I saw where the wind had uprooted the willow tree over the spring."

Cathie tore her gaze away from Rob's handsome features to look at Tad. The willow tree, that special living bridge over the spring and in some strange way a link with her childhood. Now it was gone, destroyed by the storm that had brought her Rob. Then a smile came back to her mouth. It was more than an even trade.

"I'm sorry, Cat," said Rob, gently touching her cheek. "That was a special tree. Tad told me about it."

"I don't mind, darling," she replied, turning her head to brush a kiss in his palm. "Not anymore."

CHAPTER TWELVE

SUNLIGHT SHIMMERED on the smooth surface of the jade stone, striking rainbow colors on the swirling diamond brilliants on either side of the green gem while turning the circling band into molten gold. Their simple church wedding had taken place in August and Cathie still studied her wedding rings, unable to believe her good fortune. Harvest time was already nipping at the heels of summer. School had been in session for three weeks, not sufficient time for Cathie's heart to stop leaping every time one of her students addressed her as Mrs. Douglas.

She smiled up at the Saturday morning sun. She hadn't known that loving a man could bring such utter contentment and bliss. Even during the mundane tasks of making beds, fixing meals and washing dishes, she would glance in Rob's direction and feel that rush of warmth that made their relationship so special, night or day. Her temper was still with her, rising to the forefront when some minor irritation became more than she could bear, but Rob wasn't browbeaten like Clay and gave as good as he got. And they always ended up laughing about it later, or better yet—loving.

"Cathie!" Tad's voice pulled her out of her daydream.

There was more satisfaction for her watching the slender darkly tanned boy racing across the lawn to where she was reclining on a lawn chair. His bleached brown hair was tousled by the wind, his face was streaked with dirt and perspiration, his denim jeans a series of patches and grass stains. The Tad who stopped breathlessly in front of her bore almost no resemblance to the aloof, withdrawn child who had walked into her classroom those many months ago.

"Dad wants you to help him." A happy grin split his face. There was open affection in the way his hazel eyes glowed when they looked at Cathie.

"Where is he?" she asked as she rose to her feet, glancing down at her tan slacks and hoping this help Rob wanted didn't involve a greasy tractor.

"Out in the pasture," Tad replied, reaching for her hand to hurry her along.

A sad light dimmed the brilliance of her eyes, but she quickly chased it away. Cathie still couldn't get used to walking down to the pasture and not seeing the willow tree by the spring. The little ribbon of water looked so lonely without it. Of course she hadn't told Rob that. She didn't want him to think she attached that much importance to a willow tree.

"Has something happened to one of the cows?" she asked, dodging the muddy Duchess who was rejoining Tad.

"No," Tad assured her, grinning over his shoulder with an impish twinkle in his eyes that puzzled Cathie. Usually such excitement from

Tad heralded the arrival of a baby animal, but to Cathie's knowledge there was none expected.

Tad hustled her to the barnyard, taking the short cut past the concrete water tank and out the pasture gate. Near the bottom of the hill where the spring flowed into the Boyer River, Cathie saw the red and white pickup truck parked. Tad raced ahead to join his father, who had watched Cathie's hurried progress down the hill.

"Here she is!" Tad announced, fairly dancing with excitement.

"What is all this about?" Cathie asked, puzzled by the conspiratorial look exchanged between the two. Lazily Rob's brown eyes swung back to her, then he reached out to take her hand and lead her around to the opposite side of the pickup.

Tears sprang to her eyes as she looked at the sapling lying on the ground and the open hole almost in the exact spot where the old willow had been. The sapling was a willow, too. Her voice couldn't get past the lump in her throat as she looked from the baby tree to the warm, loving light in her husband's eyes.

"It's a surprise." Tad spoke up, gazing curiously at the tears trickling down her face. "Aren't you happy?"

"Yes." A sobbing laugh finally permitted speech. "I'm very happy, Tad." She felt Rob's arm around her shoulders. "How did you know?" she asked, lifting her gaze to his face.

"Oh, Cat—" he smiled, tenderly wiping a tear from her cheek "—I saw your chin trembling the day we burnt the last of the dead limbs. I know you tried not to let me see, but I know you too well."

"Thank you," she whispered.

"I didn't do it for you, you know." The velvet eyes gleamed with mischief. "It will be years before this willow can grow big enough for you to climb. I'm planting it for our grandchildren."

Tad took no notice of the flame-colored flags in Cathie's cheeks. "We've figured it out," he said importantly, "that if we tie a string on the trunk of the sapling and anchor the string on the other side of the spring, we can make it grow across on the other side just like the old one."

"No, Tad." Cathie shook her head, wiping the tears from her face to smile down at him. "Let's not do that. You see, you can't force things to be the way they were in the past. Let's let the new tree grow the way it wants to."

Tad didn't seem too excited by her suggestion, but accepted it willingly. The gentle pressure of Rob's hand on her arm brought Cathie's face around.

"You really have given up your dreams of the future," Rob murmured, gazing into her love-starred eyes. "All those plans you made to keep everything the way it was."

"All but my dream of living the rest of my life with you," she nodded.

Neither paid any attention to the onlooking boy as their lips met in a kiss that was boundless in its pledge of love.

In 1876 Eli Haradon came to the Boyer River Valley of Iowa and erected a blacksmith and wagon shop in Sac County around which the settlement of Early, Iowa grew. The railroad was built through the county in 1881, and the town moved two miles north to it. The old town site and surrounding acerage became the Haradon farm.

Eli Haradon was my great-grandfather. The first thirteen years of my life were spent in and around the town of Early with the most memorable and precious times on the Haradon farm. There, my cousin David and I built tree houses, huts and disastrous rafts. Hours were spent sitting on the banks of the Boyer reading comic books and watching the red and white bobbers on our bamboo poles floating on the river.

This last fall, after nearly a hundred years as the family home, the farm was sold out of the Haradon family. I took a last, nostalgic journey over my beloved farm this spring. As I paused near the remains of the willow tree that once bridged the spring flowing into the Boyer, I knew this farm—my "homeplace"—must become the focal point of my novel. All the characters and incidents in this story are fictitious, but the farm is real, as are my memories of my own idyllic days where the wildest dream was no farther out of reach then the top limb of my favorite climbing tree that I long ago committed to poetry.

Janet Dailey